STAR WARS®

JEDI QUEST

BY JUDE WATSON

THE SHADOW TRAP

SCHOLASTIC INC.

New York   Toronto   London   Auckland   Sydney
Mexico City   New Delhi   Hong Kong   Buenos Aires

www.starwars.com
www.starwarskids.com
www.scholastic.com

ISBN 0-439-33922-7

Cover art by Alicia Buelow and David Mattingly.

12 11 10 9 8 7 6 5 4 3 2 1   3 4 5 6 7 8/0

Printed in the U.S.A.
First printing, May 2003

Anakin Skywalker hated being between missions. As far as he was concerned, having free time was highly overrated. How many times could he perfect his Jung Ma movement in dulon training?

Countless times, his Master, Obi-Wan Kenobi, would say.

Anakin pulled his outer tunic over his head and tossed it on the grassy bank of the lake. He took three quick steps and dived into the clear, green water. Without a mission, he just felt aimless. There was much to do at the Temple, of course. Being a Jedi meant that training never stopped. Perfecting his battle mind, bettering his grasp of galactic politics — these were all necessary tasks between missions. Usually, Anakin tried to use his time at the Temple well. But this time . . . this time, all he wanted to do was swim.

He chose a time when the lake was deserted. For some reason, this was at midday, when most Jedi students were deep in study or training, and Jedi Knights were busy as well, perfecting the ideal battle skills that Anakin should have been perfecting.

All Anakin knew was that he could not wait to dive into the cool, green water. He felt his mind calm as he swam underwater, playing with the rays of light that penetrated beneath the surface. He and his Master were not communicating well. Ever since his mission to Andara, there had been distance between them. Obi-Wan had said he was deeply disappointed in him. Although it was not in the character of a Jedi to dwell on the past, Anakin remembered that comment like a knife in his heart. It haunted every moment of their time together.

In the past he had sometimes felt irritated at Obi-Wan's corrections, his need to always show Anakin how he could have done something better, or more patiently, or more thoroughly. Now he missed them. He saw them now for what they were — a dedication to him, a need to help him be the best Jedi he could be.

Anakin broke the surface and shook off drops of water. He was close to the waterfall now, and he paused to feel the cool mist on his skin. With a few quick strokes he swam to the bank and hauled himself up to sit underneath the spray.

And, just like that, it happened.

The vision came, and the peaceful scene before him fell away. The rushing water became a rush of air so intense that it hurt his ears. Images came and went so quickly they were like pulses of light: a massive fleet at his command; a revolt of hundreds of slaves as they shouted his name; striding through the dusty streets of Mos Espa and reaching the door of his old home. The images stopped and froze only once. His mother's face as he clasped her against him. He touched the slave cuffs at her wrists and they fell to the floor. He heard the clang.

And then there was an explosion of light and sorrow, and he knew he had lost Shmi, had lost, in fact, everyone he loved, including Obi-Wan.

The One Below remains below.

Suddenly Anakin felt the grass underneath his fingers, springy and soft. He heard the sound of the waterfall. The explosion of blinding light fractured and mellowed into the cool greens of the water.

It was the third time he had had the vision. Before, it had come late at night, when he was close to sleep. The first time it had been almost a dream. The second, it had been clear and sharp. But this time it was insistent. It seemed to cling to him like a sticky web he couldn't escape.

What did it mean? Why did the vision of liberating slaves come to him? He hadn't had that thought since he was a young boy on Tatooine. He often dwelled on his mother, of course, dreamed of freeing her from her harsh life. Yet this vision was so *real.* It felt as though he really had the power to do it. He saw now the difference between a dream and a vision.

Who was The One Below?

Anakin shook his head, watching as water droplets hit the skin of his forearm. He felt troubled and weary. Swimming every day wasn't enough to clear his mind, calm his heart.

It was time to tell Obi-Wan about it.

On Andara, Obi-Wan had faulted him for acting without regard to his instructions. Anakin had known that a fellow Jedi Padawan, Ferus Olin, had disappeared. Instead of telling Obi-Wan, he had gone off with the group he was investigating. Anakin had thought that he would find Ferus by continuing with the mission. Obi-Wan had disagreed when he found out. Anakin had never seen him so angry. He had felt that Anakin had violated an essential core of trust between them.

It had not mattered at all that Ferus had been found safe, and that the mission had been successful.

It made no difference to the Jedi Council, either. Anakin had been asked to appear before the full Council and accept a reprimand, a serious failing for a Padawan. He and Obi-Wan had been on several missions since, but things between them weren't the same. They had lost a rhythm Anakin had not been sure was there, until he had lost it.

Reluctantly, Anakin slipped back into his tunic with one hand and, with the other, contacted his Master on his comlink. Obi-Wan answered immediately.

"It's Anakin. I need to speak to you about something. I don't wish to interrupt you, but —"

"I'm in the Room of the Thousand Fountains."

"I'll be there in a few minutes, then."

Anakin shoved his comlink back into his belt. He couldn't remember the last time he'd felt free to tease his Master, or the last time Obi-Wan had made a joke. Lately he'd begun to wonder if Obi-Wan still wanted him as his Padawan at all. It was not unheard of for a Master to step away. Unusual, yes, but not every pairing was the right one. It was considered no shame on the Padawan if a more appropriate Master was needed. But Anakin would feel the shame.

The Room of the Thousand Fountains wasn't far from the lake. He hurried down the wooded trail. Illumination banks overhead created an impression of sunlight streaming through the green leaves. Anakin wished he could enjoy the peace that the Jedi found on these shores.

His Master was sitting on a favorite bench, his eyes closed. No doubt he was meditating or listening to the fountains that were often compared to the delicate chiming of bells.

Without opening his eyes, his Master spoke. "You sounded disturbed."

Anakin sat next to him. Obi-Wan opened his eyes and sent him a penetrating glance. "I've had a vision," Anakin said. "It's come three times, and I need to make sense of it."

"Visions do not always make sense." Obi-Wan swung around to face Anakin. "Tell me about it."

Anakin outlined the vision. It was still so clear in his head that he had no trouble remembering the details.

"The One Below remains below," Obi-Wan murmured.

"Do you know what that means?"

Obi-Wan didn't answer. "Yoda should hear about this."

"Hear about what, I wonder," Yoda called, heading toward them and leaning on his gimer stick. "To find you, I come, Obi-Wan. Expecting a problem, I was not."

Obi-Wan smiled as he rose. "Not a problem. A vision has been troubling Anakin."

"A vision, you say?" Yoda swiveled to fix Anakin with a curious look. He settled himself on a rock and rested his hands on top of his stick, his posture for listening.

Once again, Anakin related the vision, leaving out his feelings about it. He knew that Yoda would want to know only the details.

Strangely, Yoda repeated the same thing that Obi-Wan had. "The One Below remains below," he murmured.

"Do you know who that is, Master Yoda?" Anakin asked.

Yoda nodded slowly. "Know her well, I do. Master Yaddle, it is."

"Master Yaddle was imprisoned for centuries on the world of Koda," Obi-Wan explained. "The Kodans gave her that name, The One Below."

Anakin nodded. He had known about Yaddle's long imprisonment, but he had never heard that name. Yaddle was the same species as Yoda, and sat on the Jedi Council. She was a revered Jedi Master. He was surprised that she'd been a part of his vision.

"About to leave on a mission to Mawan, she is," Yoda said. "A troubling one, I fear. Debated, we have, which Jedi team to send with her. The answer, perhaps your vision is."

Anakin felt a rush of disappointment. He realized at that moment that he had been hoping that the vision meant he needed to travel to Tatooine. He had imagined that he would be able to step out of his dreams and free his mother in reality. "I thought perhaps the vision meant I could somehow help the slaves on Tatooine," he said hesitantly.

Yoda and Obi-Wan both shook their heads.

"Careful you must be. Difficult to interpret, visions are," Yoda said. "A map, a vision is not."

Anakin hid his impatience. Wasn't Yoda interpreting his vision for him, and telling him where he needed to go?

Obi-Wan sensed his confusion. "Visions of freeing slaves are not surprising," he told Anakin. "That desire rests deep within you. It is natural that it would rise up in some form. To follow a vision literally is often a mistake."

"But isn't following Yaddle also literal?" Anakin asked.

Yoda made a slight gesture with his gimer stick, an acknowledgment of Anakin's point. "A warning, the vision is." He turned to Obi-Wan. "Grave, the situation on Mawan has become."

Obi-Wan nodded. "It is a sad situation. I knew the planet when it was thriving."

"Open now, this world is," Yoda said.

"Open?" Anakin asked.

"Mawan was torn apart by a civil war ten years ago," Obi-Wan explained. "The planet was decimated by the conflict and was never able to set up a government afterward. The capital city completely lost its infrastructure — its roads deteriorated, its space lanes went unmonitored, and finally its power grid went down completely. Much of the housing was destroyed, too. A majority of the citizens were left jobless and homeless. Many moved to the country, but a famine devastated the population there. The absence of government, security, and hope left a void that criminal elements rushed in to fill. It's now an open world, where anything can happen without fear of the law. Criminals from throughout the galaxy have set up operations there. There is no safety for the citizens."

"Too busy, the Senate has been," Yoda said. "But ignore Mawan, they can no longer. Ripples of evil, open worlds have. Affect the galaxy, they do. Asked the Senate has for a Jedi presence to help establish a provisional government committee. To have the trust of the Mawans, a diplomat we need."

"A diplomat, yes, but also a warrior," Obi-Wan remarked. "Someone who can convince the criminal gangs that it is in their best interest to leave the planet. I can see why you chose Yaddle."

Yoda inclined his head. "Our most able diplomat, she is. Accomplished in the ways of the Force. But assistance she needs. Help her, you and your Padawan must, for important this mission is. As goes Mawan, so go other worlds. Growing in the galaxy, the dark side is."

"We are ready, Master Yoda," Obi-Wan said.

Anakin nodded. But he felt a dread he did not understand. Even hearing the name of the planet had created a sour feeling in his stomach. Usually a mission excited him, no matter how difficult or dangerous. Yet he knew that he did not want to go to Mawan.

CHAPTER TWO

The Republic cruiser flew low over Mawan's capital city of Naatan. Obi-Wan leaned closer to look out the cockpit window. The power grid was being fought over by the crimelords, and had been repeatedly damaged in successive raids and takeovers. Tonight the grid was down and the city was black. It rose out of the night like a dark shadow.

He had flown into Naatan at night before. Years ago, before the war. The city had glowed from kilometers above in space. The Mawans were fond of soft colors, which they used to filter the harsh light of their world. They used delicate rose lights to illuminate their streets and plazas at night, and from the air the city had glowed like a rare pink jewel.

He had always enjoyed his visits to Naatan. The city

had been a thriving cosmopolitan center. It had been an important stop on the primary Core trade route, and the wealth of the city had spread to its parks, libraries, and schools.

As they flew lower, dipping down into an unused space lane, he could see that those parks were now black holes in the landscape, as painful as wounds. The schools were now in ruins, the libraries leveled. Obi-Wan saw broken windows, twisted gates, half-demolished cafés. Abandoned speeders left on the street. Everywhere he looked, Obi-Wan saw desolation. It wasn't just the property, it was what the property represented — the ruin of so many lives, busy lives that had been lived in pleasant surroundings. Now those lives had been driven underground, and evil had moved into the vacuum.

"Gone underground," Euraana Fall said. "The only ones who remain are part of the criminal gangs." A native of Naatan, Euraana had the delicate, pale skin and blue veins that were prized by the Mawan. Mawans had two hearts and their blue veins lay close to their skin, a mark of beauty on the planet. Euraana's grief showed in her shimmering gray eyes, but her voice was steady. "Most of the citizens live in the infrastructure tunnels. Before the Great Purge — what Mawans call the civil war — all of our goods were transported below the city, in tunnels, and airlifted to the surface. Our computer centers and control links are there, too. It's what made the city so pleasant. For a busy city, we had little traffic."

"Yes, it was a wonderful city to stroll in," Obi-Wan said as the craft neared landing. "Your cafés and restaurants were always full of talk and music."

"And our parks held the laughter of our children," Euraana agreed, her gaze quietly sweeping over the city. "All gone." She pointed in the distance. "There is the quarter where the crimelord Striker rules. He is known by that name because of the projectile pistols his gang used for their first raid. Strikers are not sophisticated weapons, but they won the battle. Now they are better armed, of course. He is reputed to have the most extensive weapons cache of all the crimelords."

Obi-Wan leaned over to look at the quarter of the city that Euraana had indicated. Garish blue and green glowlights were hung from poles to cast their eerie light on the streets. Half-destroyed buildings were rebuilt with inexpensive, brightly colored plastoid materials. The replacements were slapped onto old buildings built of polished stone, making a tawdry contrast. This quarter did have a few beings in its streets, with state-of-the-art speeders sporting shiny paint and flashing lights moving through the streets and cafés full of beings. It was obvious that there was trading going on. The progress of their transport was watched with calculating eyes.

"What are they buying and selling?" Anakin asked.

Euraana shrugged. "Weapons. Spice. Illegal medicines they will sell to the unfortunates in the galaxy. Fortunes are being made down there. And those fortunes are built on the ashes of our civilization."

"No longer," Yaddle said softly. She had talked little on the journey and had spent much of it meditating. Now the sharp gaze from her green-brown eyes seemed to give strength to Euraana, who nodded. Although Yaddle was small in size, her presence loomed large.

Without air traffic guidelines, the Senate pilot didn't need clearance or coordinates. The landing platforms for the city had all been destroyed. He set the cruiser down in a large courtyard of a formerly impressive living complex, carefully avoiding the rubble.

Obi-Wan watched Anakin as his Padawan grabbed his survival pack and waited with the others for the ramp to lower. Usually at the start of a new mission Anakin's eyes were alive with curiosity. Obi-Wan had always appreciated how his Padawan threw himself into a new situation, using all of his senses to gather information. But Anakin's expression looked shuttered.

He walked beside him as they exited the craft. "Any impressions?" He was always interested to hear what

Anakin had picked up. The Force spoke to Anakin in a different way than anyone Obi-Wan had ever known.

Anakin shook his head. "Nothing to speak of. I feel the dark side of the Force, of course. That's clear."

"And to be expected," Obi-Wan said. "What about your vision? Any connections?"

Anakin shook his head. "Nothing."

There were shadows between them now. He could see them in the way Anakin held his shoulders, the way his eyes spoke. It wasn't as though Anakin didn't meet his gaze directly. But his gaze was like glass. Obi-Wan found himself sliding off it into uncertainty.

He knew he was partly responsible. Ever since Andara he had held himself back from his Padawan. His anger had gone, but it had been replaced with caution. He had wanted to give Anakin room, time to reflect without the pressure of his own opinions and interpretations. He knew he could be heavy-handed at times. He remembered Qui-Gon, how his own Master had sometimes withdrawn his focus on him and gone to a place Obi-Wan could not reach. It had sometimes left Obi-Wan feeling stranded, but it had forced him to come to terms with his own feelings. He wanted to do the same for Anakin. His Padawan was sixteen now. It was time for him to achieve a deeper connection to his core.

Anakin had been wrong on Andara. The fact that he

had concealed the disappearance of a Jedi still astonished Obi-Wan. His actions did not take away from the fact that Anakin was special. When he made mistakes, they were big ones. His need to be perfect, to be powerful, was a flaw. Try as he might, Obi-Wan could not show Anakin that if he held himself back, everything would come to him. Anakin just kept pushing.

He resolved to work out some of their differences on this mission. They were on a journey together, and for each phase they would develop different rhythms, different paces. Anakin needed to understand that. A little distance between them didn't mean that the core was threatened.

"Our contacts are meeting us nearby," Euraana Fall said. "This way."

The Jedi picked their way through the rubble of the courtyard and followed Euraana down the dark street, leaving the pilot and cruiser behind. "Better not use a glow rod," she said. "No need to attract attention. This part of the city isn't used much. It will be a good place for us to set up operations."

She led them to a building that seemed miraculously untouched by the signs of war, until they entered and saw that part of the rear portion had been blown out. The domed ceiling was half destroyed. Stars littered the sky above, thrown like mineral dust on shim-mersilk.

"This was once a meeting hall." Euraana's voice echoed in the space. "I attended lectures here, and concerts. There are still offices and even a café here. We can make it work."

Two forms separated from the shadows. Obi-Wan tensed, but he saw almost immediately that they were friendly. They were most likely the Mawan contacts. They were both short, muscular men with pale com-plexions and long hair that was tied back with metal clasps. One of the men had gleaming dark hair, the other snowy white.

The shorter one with the white hair and youthful face gave a short nod to Euraana and held out his hand, palm out, in the Mawan gesture of friendship and welcome. "Glad to see you made it." His voice rumbled like a balky sublight engine.

"Greetings to you, Swanny," Euraana said to the white-haired man. Then she faced the dark-haired Mawan and said, "Hello, Rorq." Euraana turned and in-troduced the two to the Jedi party. The two men nodded greetings.

"Swanny and Rorq were tunnel workers before the war," Euraana explained. "They live below. The tunnel workers have agreed to help us, and they are their representatives."

"I'm afraid I haven't been thoroughly briefed," Obi-Wan said politely. "Tunnel workers?"

Swanny bristled. "What's wrong with that?"

Euraana said quickly, "Let me explain. Before the war, the tunnel workers were . . . well, near the bottom of the social structure —"

"Meaning the high-and-mighties looked down on us," Rorq said, crossing his thick arms. "Called us subrats."

"Even though we kept everything running for them," Swanny added with a cynical twist to his mouth.

"So the order of things," Euraana said, holding her hand up and flipping it over, "is now reversed."

"Subrats on top," Swanny said. "It's a sweet thing."

"The citizens below depend on the tunnel workers to bring provisions and keep their generators going," Euraana continued. "They have practically fashioned a city down below."

"We saved their hides," Rorq growled.

"We've gotten a taste of power, and we like it," Swanny said. "Not only that, we're good at it. So we'd like to be involved in the rebuilding of Naatan. Not from the bottom, though. Things have changed."

"Everything has changed," Euraana said quietly.

"Before the Purge, Euraana here wouldn't have

given me the time of day," Swanny said. "Now she has to deal with me."

"Oh?" Euraana said, cocking an eyebrow. "Do you know me so well, Swanny Mull? Enough to call me a snob and an opportunist in one breath?"

Swanny grinned and held up his hands. "Maybe I spoke too soon."

"Maybe you should stick to things you know about," Euraana snapped in a tart tone. "The crimelords, for example." She turned to the others. "The tunnel workers serve as go-betweens. The citizens are forced to buy their food and goods from the crimelords in temporary markets set up below in the tunnels. The tunnel workers set it up." She gave Swanny an icy glance. "They are paid by the crimelords for their services, as well as by the citizens."

"Why shouldn't we be paid?" Swanny asked mildly. "We take the risks."

"Tell us about the crimelords," Obi-Wan said. If he didn't step in, he had a feeling Euraana and Swanny would trade taunts for hours. "Who is the most dangerous? Who is the most powerful? Sometimes they aren't one and the same."

Swanny frowned. "Most of the criminals in Naatan are low-level types working for bosses. I'd say your three biggest problems are Striker, Feeana Tala, and Decca."

"Let's start with Decca," Obi-Wan said.

"She's a Hutt," Rorq said with a shudder. "The daughter of Gardulla. Decca took over Gardulla's organization when she died. Her center of operations used to be on C-Foroon, near Tatooine, but she got chased off. She came here and brought her goons with her. She's mainly in the spice trade."

"But she has a personal grudge against Striker," Swanny said. "He hit her operation within days of arriving on Mawan. Grabbed control of the power grid and a warehouse full of weapons. But Decca's got the edge in transport. She controls most of the main tunnels. She stole most of Naatan's transports when she arrived and she's managed to hold on to them."

"The only trouble is, she doesn't have fuel for them," Rorq said. "Striker keeps raiding her fuel supplies, just to make her angry. He doesn't need that much fuel. He doesn't have as many transports."

"Nobody knows who Striker is?" Anakin asked.

Swanny shook his head. "Not many have even seen him. His operators were in control for years, and he only dropped in from time to time. But he's been spending all of his time here lately." He nodded at Obi-Wan. "I'd say he was the most powerful. And dangerous."

"And Feeana Tala?" Yaddle asked. "A native of Mawan, she is."

Rorq nodded. "She controls most of the goods and services that are sold to the citizens below. Small potatoes for the other crimelords."

"Still, they raid her when they feel like it," Swanny said. "They want to control as much of what happens on Mawan as they can. Decca wants Striker off-planet, and he wants the same for her. Feeana's edge is that she knows the tunnels below almost as well as we do."

Euraana looked at Yaddle. "So what is our first step?"

"Return and take back the city, the citizens must," Yaddle said. "So control of the power grid we must have."

"You'll have to guarantee their safety," Euraana said.

Yaddle turned to her and blinked in a gesture that was very much like Yoda's. "Guarantee, you say? Guarantees, there never are." She spread her hands. "Help them we will. Courage must they find themselves."

Euraana nodded. "If we can get the power grid back, we might be able to persuade them to leave the tunnels. And if there was at least some progress with the crimelords —"

"That is our job," Obi-Wan said, indicating himself and Anakin. "They must be told that if they don't voluntarily leave the planet, Senate security forces will make them go."

"If the Senate will send them," Euraana said worriedly. "They still have not agreed."

"Agree they will, if take back the city we can," Yaddle said.

"What if the crimelords don't listen to talk?" Swanny asked. "In my experience, they seldom do."

"We have to find a reason to make them listen," Obi-Wan said. "Everyone is vulnerable somewhere. For now we just need to learn more about their operations."

"Swanny and Rorq can help you there," Euraana said. "Aboveground has been so destroyed that even the crimelords have bunkers belowground."

"Safer down there in case something bad happens," Swanny said. He grinned at Obi-Wan and Anakin. "We know just about everything that goes on down there."

"Take us below," Obi-Wan said. "We'll be in touch while you take care of the power grid," he said to Yaddle. Yaddle nodded good-bye.

"If you'll follow me." Swanny gave a bow to the Jedi that held a hint of mockery.

Obi-Wan and Anakin strode after the two. Obi-Wan's instincts were on alert. He had his doubts about the value of Swanny and Rorq's assistance. They were scruffy, rude, and probably untrustworthy.

Qui-Gon would have befriended them instantly.

CHAPTER THREE

Anakin walked with Obi-Wan, following Swanny through the dark streets to an industrial part of Naatan, an area made even darker by the presence of the shells of unlighted buildings looming overhead. Swanny led them to a booth that was a tall cylinder made of opaque black glass in a passage between two former warehouses.

"This is a forced air tube," Swanny said. "We use them instead of turbolifts. If you've never been on one, it can feel a little strange. You step out on air, and the pressure lessens, dropping you below." He opened a control panel and punched in a level and a speed. "I'll keep it slow for your first time. Just don't ever turn the control to 'eject.' That's what we used to get rid of toxic substances — we'd just blast them into the atmosphere. The roof of the cylinder retracts, and you'd find yourself lost in the clouds."

"Are there many levels below?" Obi-Wan asked.

"About twenty," Rorq said. "And the tunnels extend over the entire area of Naatan. It's like another city down there. You'll see."

Rorq stepped into the air tube with no floor. He hung there for a second, grinning at them, then shot below.

Swanny gestured. "After you."

Obi-Wan stepped out into what seemed to be a black void. Anakin heard the faint sound of rushing air. The next thing he knew, his Master had sunk down out of sight.

"Next," Swanny said.

Anakin stepped into the chamber. It felt strange to feel the air pressure against his boots. He descended, the air rushing against his ears. The sensation felt oddly familiar, even though he'd never been in an airlift before. When he reached the bottom he felt the shock of the ground against his boots and almost stumbled as he stepped off.

Obi-Wan and Rorq were waiting. After a moment, Swanny joined them, stepping off the airlift with the ease of long practice.

"Ah," Swanny said, spreading his arms to take in the dim, dirty tunnel, "home, sweet home."

Anakin wrinkled his nose. The air was dank and heavy and smelled stale.

Swanny grinned. "The purification system is hooked into the power grid. Sometimes it's off, sometimes it's on. Lately it's been off."

Swanny activated a glow rod and they set off down the tunnel. It was wide and high, big enough for the four of them to walk side by side.

"This is one of the main transport tunnels," Swanny explained. "We used to have speeders operating along here. Now we motor the old-fashioned way."

Obi-Wan glanced around at the network of tunnels branching off from the one they were walking down. "I don't know how you keep from getting lost."

"There are map kiosks, but when the power's down, we can't access them," Rorq said. "Luckily, we could find our way around down here blindfolded. Patrol, Swanny."

Quickly, Swanny deactivated the glow rod. Rorq dived into a side tunnel and Swanny urged them through the opening. They pressed against the walls of the side tunnel as a speeder slowly made its way down the main tunnel. Two guards sat, blaster rifles at the ready.

"Better to avoid them," Swanny whispered. "Decca's crew."

"Does she run patrols frequently?" Obi-Wan asked.

"I'd say randomly," Swanny said. "She doesn't have enough fuel for regular patrols, so she counts on surprise. She's always looking to round up some of Striker's men if she can. They capture you and ask questions later. I'd rather avoid a rifle butt on the scalp, thank you."

They walked back into the main tunnel. "The substations are where the main computer relays used to be," Swanny said, holding the glow rod high so that they could pick their way down the tunnel. "Most of them have been destroyed in blaster shoot-'em-up battles. There are also docking bays for our once-gleaming fleet of transports. Decca controls most of the docking bays. And the rest of the crimelords have taken over most of the substations."

"Where do the Mawans live?" Anakin asked.

"They took over a half-dug-out area that was supposed to be another loading bay before the Purge. They set up a kind of tent village there. We subrats serve as scouts to protect them from raids. We also ferry food, water, and other supplies."

"For a fee," Obi-Wan said.

Swanny nodded. "A small fee, just to cover costs. We have to pay bribes to the crimelords."

"Who controls the power grid now?" Obi-Wan asked.

"Striker, at the moment," Swanny said. "That could change. The main generator is in a substation down here. Striker has it guarded."

"Can't you switch power from the main substation to another?" Anakin asked.

Swanny shrugged. "Technically, yes. But it's not easy. They'll need a lot of luck to boost the system from another source. Plus there's a relay substation that will shut the whole system down if procedure isn't followed. Nobody wants to do that, even the crimelords. Too much risk that the entire system would never restart. They all want to control the power grid. They don't want to destroy it."

"What did you do before the Purge, Swanny?" Obi-Wan asked.

"I'm a water rat," Swanny said cheerfully. "I programmed all the wastewater systems. I know every pipe down here, just about. Rorq here was on fuel transport tunnels."

"Barely got paid a living wage to keep the surface running," Rorq grumbled.

Swanny clapped an arm around Rorq's shoulders. "Ah, but it was a sweet life, wasn't it, my friend? Low life expectancy, no bonuses, the contempt of our fellow citizens — you've got to admit, you miss it."

Rorq shook his head. "You're crazy."

"That's why I'm happy," Swanny said with a twisted grin. "How else do I stay sane?"

"Why are you working with us?" Obi-Wan asked curiously. "If the citizens take back Naatan, there's every chance you could end up underground again."

"True words," Swanny said. "Most of the tunnel workers are hanging back. They won't give their support. They like the power they have, even if they're operating under a corrupt system that could get them killed at any moment. Call me crazy, but I want to live long enough to see the sun again. Naatan will be returned to the Mawans one day. I'm sure of that. If I help the right people, I'll be rewarded." He grinned. "Just call me a visionary with a deep interest in my own well-being."

"If you like," Obi-Wan said.

Anakin could see by the expression on Obi-Wan's face that his Master was amused by Swanny. It never failed to surprise him when his proper Master loosened up with some sort of odd character.

"Now, where would you Jedi like to start?" Swanny asked. "Naturally, Rorq and myself would prefer to keep ourselves out of any extremely dangerous scenarios, but we're ready for almost anything."

"We need to observe the systems they've set up, how they operate," Obi-Wan said. "I don't want them to know the Jedi are here, not yet. It doesn't pay to present a deal until you know what's important to your adversary."

Rorq looked nervous. "You mean infiltrate their hideouts?"

"Unless you can think of another way," Obi-Wan said.

"Down, boy," Swanny said absently to Rorq. His eyes narrowed as he thought, and he stopped walking. "We arrange temporary markets for Feeana. Set up a time and place for the Mawans to buy and trade. There's one tonight. She's the one who deals with us most often. Doesn't cheat the Mawans quite as much as the others. If you keep your hoods over your faces and don't attract attention to yourselves, you could pass for Mawans. Feeana will probably be there. She likes to keep an eye on things."

Obi-Wan nodded. "Let's go."

Swanny and Rorq led them through the maze of tunnels, walking fast and purposefully now. They descended several levels and twisted through a small network of tunnels that suddenly opened out into a large space.

It had once been used for storage, that was clear. Open shelving was built into the curving durasteel wall frames. Plastoid bins lined one wall. Everything was empty. Instead, blankets were spread out on the scuffed floor of the space, and a ragtag assortment of items were spread out. Fruit that was past its prime, flour, some battered kitchen items, a broken warming unit. Folded thermal capes, their edges ragged and torn. An old pair of boots.

The Mawans wandered among the goods. Anakin saw how their eyes lingered hungrily on the different items, how their hands dangled uselessly by their sides or how they fingered empty purses hung on belts. The last time he had seen such hopelessness had been in the slave quarters on Tatooine.

"They can't afford anything, but they come anyway," Swanny said.

Bored gang members, blaster rifles in their hands, stood against the walls, some leaning and trying not to doze.

Across the space a Mawan female sat astride a battered durasteel box, her hand resting lightly on her blaster holster. She was younger than Anakin had imagined, about Obi-Wan's age, he guessed, and she looked wiry and tough. She wore a comlink headset and spoke rapidly into it while her eyes scanned the room. Anakin kept his hood forward to conceal his face. Without the telltale blue veins of a Mawan, he would be identified immediately as an outsider.

He and Obi-Wan kept their heads down and shuffled along with the others. Anakin knew his Master was trying to get closer, hoping to overhear whatever directions Feeana was giving on her headset.

He looked at her with a sidelong glance and saw how sharply she was watching the crowd. Her gaze slowly dropped, and suddenly, she stood and leaped. The strength and power of the leap surprised him. She landed only centimeters away from him and Obi-Wan.

"Spies!" she cried, her blaster leveled at Obi-Wan's chest. "Surround them!"

CHAPTER FOUR

Feeana's quick action didn't extend to her troops. A leader with a headset sputtered toward them, trying to corral others to follow. Anakin knew that his Master could have foiled them in seconds, but he waited for them to approach. Soon they were surrounded by twenty members of Feeana's gang, and twenty blasters were pointed in their direction.

Anakin glanced at his Master. Obi-Wan said nothing. His gaze was calm and watchful. Anakin knew his Master's strategy usually centered on waiting. Obi-Wan could strike faster than any Jedi he knew, but he could also wait longer than any Jedi should have to, in Anakin's opinion. Especially when a blaster was pointed at his heart.

Still, he was an apprentice, and his job was to follow his Master's lead.

"You're from Decca's gang," Feeana said. "Don't bother denying it."

Feeana whirled toward Swanny and Rorq, who were both backing away with careful steps.

"Swanny and Rorq brought them," she said.

Immediately, ten of the twenty blasters turned on Swanny and Rorq.

"Whoa," Swanny said, holding up two hands while Rorq bared his teeth in a nervous grin. "We just walked in at the same time."

"Never saw them before in our lives," Rorq said through clenched teeth.

"We're not spies," Obi-Wan said. "We're Jedi. We're here for diplomacy, not battles."

"Prove it," Feeana sneered.

Only by a small expression did Obi-Wan reveal how annoyed he was at the request. He put out a hand, and Feeana's headset flew off her head and directly into his grasp.

Obi-Wan spoke crisply into the headset. "Cancel all orders. Take a vacation."

The gang members looked at one another. The leader of the group, who was wearing a comlink headpiece, put a hand to his ear, as if unable to quite believe that Obi-Wan had just given an order.

Anakin could hear confused exclamations and questions faintly coming from the headpiece in Obi-Wan's hand. He suppressed his grin.

Feeana tilted her head in a short nod of appreciation. "Okay, you're a Jedi. Now, can I have my comlink back? They're hard to come by."

Obi-Wan tossed it to her. Feeana spoke into it. "Hold your positions until further notice." She glanced at the Jedi. "So you're here for diplomacy. Let's talk."

Feeana led the way to a corner. She pulled up a durasteel bin and overturned another for a makeshift seating area. Then she motioned to the Jedi to sit down. She looked at Obi-Wan expectantly.

"The Senate has sent a Provisional Government Committee for Mawan," Obi-Wan said. "They are aboveground right now. Senate security forces are expected within a matter of days."

"In other words, they're finally going to do something," Feeana said.

"Yes," Obi-Wan said. "Mawan cannot remain an open world. After the crimelords are put out of business, the Senate will arrange for a transfer of power to the Mawans."

Feeana put her hands on her hips. "So what do you want from me?"

"We hope that the crimelords will voluntarily either dissolve their gangs or move off-planet," Obi-Wan said. "Your choice. There's no other."

"And what do I get?" Feeana asked.

"You get to avoid going up against the Jedi and an extremely well-armed security force," Obi-Wan said.

Feeana gave him a shrewd look. "You'll have to come up with something better than that, Jedi. Surely you know that deals have high stakes when one side has nothing to lose."

"Why don't you tell me what you want?" Obi-Wan suggested. "It will save time."

Anakin admired his Master's cool. Obi-Wan seemed to know what Feeana was thinking. He himself had no idea.

"Amnesty," Feeana said. "I'm a native Mawan. I don't want to go off-planet. I'm not really a crimelord. Think of me as a thief who does well. And you tell me what other choice I had. Because of the greedy leadership of my government, I lost my home. I was forced underground. At first, I stole to feed my family. Then I stole to feed other families. Then I needed a cut of what I stole in order to keep stealing. Then I needed a few others to help. Before I knew it I had a gang. I supply the Mawans with what they need to survive. Without me they'd be at the mercy of Decca and Striker. At least I am loyal to Mawan. I am a Mawan first, a criminal second. Amnesty shouldn't be hard to give."

"I think that can be arranged," Obi-Wan agreed. "What else?"

"A promise," Feeana said. "No doubt this Provisional Committee will be involved in setting up the Mawan government. Insiders will get the best jobs. I want to be part of that group."

"A moment," Obi-Wan said. He stepped away to activate his comlink. Anakin watched as he spoke quietly into it. Then he returned and nodded at Feeana. "Your request is granted. And in return, you are expected to move to the surface with your group to serve as a temporary security force while the Provisional Committee works on getting control of the power grid."

"Hold that comlink," Feeana said. "I'm not doing anything until I'm sure you're going to succeed."

"I don't think you're in a position to make demands," Obi-Wan said. "You have to earn your amnesty by proving your loyalty to your homeworld. Didn't you just say you were a Mawan first, or am I mistaken? And if I were you, I'd want to make a generous gesture that will win you support later."

He held her gaze. Anakin watched the battle of wills. He had no doubt who would win.

"All right," Feeana agreed at last. "I'll do it."

She moved off to speak into her comlink. Anakin let go of the breath he didn't realize he was holding.

"One down," he murmured to Obi-Wan.

Obi-Wan gazed after Feeana. "Maybe. We'll have to move fast to keep her loyalty. If she feels we might lose control of Naatan, she'll go back on the deal. We have to neutralize Decca and Striker, and fast."

CHAPTER FIVE

Swanny and Rorq rushed across the hall. "My friend, that was a sweet thing to watch," Swanny congratulated him. "You stared down Feeana and won. If I had a hat, it would be off to you."

"Excellent diplomacy," Rorq echoed in a gush of obvious flattery. "I learned a lot just watching you."

"Thanks," Obi-Wan said dryly. "Your support means a lot."

"Anytime," Swanny assured him.

"Particularly for the part where you pretended not to know us," Obi-Wan added.

"What can I say?" Swanny said. "My survival mechanism just kicked in. I run on instinct. Can't control it. I want to be brave, but something happens, and I open my mouth and a womp weasel starts talking. Nothing personal."

"Sure," Obi-Wan said. "But you owe me one."

Swanny and Rorq looked nervous. "And what would that 'one' be?" Swanny asked cautiously.

"Help us infiltrate Decca's camp," Obi-Wan said. "That means you come, too. If I know Hutts, we won't be able to bargain the way we did with Feeana. Decca won't willingly agree to vacate the planet. We'll have to find the flaw in her organization, some way to smash it, or at least make things too difficult for her to stick around. That means we have to get right in the middle of things and see how they're done."

"We can certainly give you the location of Decca's camp," Swanny said. "That is no problem."

"And your awesome Jedi skills would no doubt allow you to smuggle yourself in," Rorq added helpfully.

Obi-Wan just waited.

"I can see that you are looking for more from us," Swanny said.

"Which you already promised," Obi-Wan said. "Unless you'd like to take this up with the Provisional Committee."

"Noooo," Swanny said, drawing the word out. "Don't think I'd want to do that. Maybe there is a way to get you inside. There's a revel tonight."

"A revel?" Anakin asked.

"Decca won a skirmish today with Striker," Swanny

said. "She always throws a big party so her gang can celebrate. Food, drink, music . . . and that's where Rorq and I come in. I just have one question."

Obi-Wan and Anakin waited.

"Can you sing?" Swanny asked.

The band was called Swanny and the Rooters. Swanny told the Jedi that they had played at many of Decca's revels. If they showed up at this one, Decca would assume that someone from her gang had booked them. They would be taking a chance, but not a very big one.

Obi-Wan and Anakin had to take the place of the other two band members. Swanny handed Obi-Wan a vioflute and Anakin a keyboard.

"Just fake it," he told them. "I'm so good no one will notice you can't play."

They set up in a corner of the vast substation while swaggering beings from all over the galaxy chugged flameouts while feasting on meat and pastries. A Whipid, his fur matted with sweat and chunks of food, handed two mugs of grog to a Kamarian, who rested one on his tusk and downed the other.

"Fun crowd," Anakin muttered to Obi-Wan.

"Just what I was thinking," Obi-Wan said through his teeth. He settled onto a stool, resting the vioflute uneasily against his shoulder. It had been surprisingly easy to crash the party — but that didn't mean the rest would be easy.

Anakin sat next to him, holding his handheld keyboard. He would have to pretend to play it. Swanny and Rorq needed backup singers, however.

"Just a few 'whee-whoas' on the choruses," Swanny swiveled around to tell them. "No solos or anything. You can follow along, can't you?"

"Of course," Obi-Wan assured him.

Swanny and Rorq ripped into a lively song, and Anakin's foot began to tap. He was surprised to find that they were good musicians.

Swanny winked at him. "Wastewater is my life, but music is a close second."

Decca the Hutt entered the room and heaved her enormous bulk onto a repulsorlift platform obviously crafted for her, large and low and festooned with shimmersilk pillows. Her lieutenants surrounded her, jockeying for position as she settled herself in. There were three, one of them a Kamarian who sat at her right, obviously her most trusted assistant. His two tails waved as he leaned over to speak directly in her ear.

"I wish we could hear what he's saying," Obi-Wan murmured, pretending to pluck the strings on his vioflute.

"Sing," Swanny hissed as he and Rorq swung into the chorus.

Anakin began to hum the backup, and beside him, Obi-Wan joined in. Unfortunately, Obi-Wan could not manage to find the melody. Swanny shot him a horrified look.

"Uh, not so loud," he hissed. "Maybe you shouldn't sing, after all."

Anakin hid his smile. He was glad his Master wasn't good at *everything*.

"Look in the corner behind Decca," Obi-Wan said to Anakin under his breath. "There's a bank of datapads. I wonder if we could get close enough to take a look at what's on them."

"If she keeps downing those flameouts, we might," Anakin said.

"Notice how she's listening to the Kamarian, while the Ranat tries to get closer."

Anakin watched. The Kamarian adjusted the pillows for Decca with his four arms while he spoke. He had Decca's full attention. It was almost comical the way the meter-tall Ranat tried to nestle into the folds of Decca's fat in order to hear what was being said.

Anakin wasn't sure what conclusions to draw from what he saw. But he knew that later his Master would ask him about his observations, so he watched carefully as Decca conferred and nodded. Then he slowly gazed around the room, noting the side tunnels and the placement of guards. He estimated there must be at least forty gang members at the party, which meant there were others on the surface and serving as guards. But how many? No doubt during their break they would be able to mingle in the crowd.

Decca signaled to Swanny, and he stopped playing. Decca held out her huge arms. Her flesh trembled. The substation fell silent.

"We hear the Jedi have arrived on Mawan with a Provisional Committee from the Senate," Decca pronounced. "Foolish beings — they think they can get rid of us."

The gang soldiers laughed and pounded the hilts of their blaster rifles on the floor.

"They will regret coming up against Decca the Hutt. I vow to you today, no committee will blast me off this planet!" Decca suddenly stood, her flesh waving. "Tell the galaxy — Decca will never retreat!"

"Well, I didn't think diplomacy would work for Decca, anyway," Obi-Wan muttered. "Let's mingle. We'll look for an opening to get to that datapad bank."

Anakin had been hoping for a chance to hit the food table. His last meal had been a protein pack on the transport. What his teachers at the Temple had seemed to leave out of their lessons was that on missions, you never got enough food. He placed his keyboard on the floor.

At that moment, an explosion blew them both off their stools. Smoke filled the substation. The ping of blaster fire suddenly filled the air.

"Stay down!" Obi-Wan shouted to Anakin. "We're under attack!"

CHAPTER SIX

The smoke was so thick and acrid that Obi-Wan's eyes streamed tears. All he could glimpse through the haze was the blur of movement and the flash of blaster fire. Hoarse shouting and battle cries almost smothered the sound of Swanny shouting, "Whoa, show's over!"

He leaned closer to Anakin. "This could be an opportunity for us," he said rapidly. "No doubt Decca has an escape plan for just this kind of attack. She'll take off and we might be able to get to those datapads. Use the Force to guide you through the smoke."

Keeping his head low, he threw himself into the brawl. Decca's gang members were literally fighting blind, their eyes screwed shut and streaming tears. This didn't stop them from firing their weapons, however. Blaster fire pinged and ricocheted around the room. Obi-Wan glided through the forest of arms and legs, allowing the Force to tell him when to raise his lightsaber to deflect fire. He sensed that the rival gang was moving steadily toward Decca, trying to get to her before she escaped. Obi-Wan had no doubt that Striker was behind the attack, most likely in retaliation for Decca's victory earlier that day.

The barrage of fire was constant, shrieking by his ears and filling the room with more sparks and heat. Electrojabbers waved in the air, and he saw one land by accident on another member of Decca's gang who was firing his blaster rifle in the air. The gang member went down, his legs paralyzed for a good two hours or more. He managed to drag himself away from a Phlog who was stomping toward the blaster fire, swinging a vibro-ax. Screams and battle cries filled the air.

It was a demonstration of sloppy fighting, Obi-Wan judged. Decca's gang might be large and fierce, but it certainly wasn't organized. Striker's soldiers were more efficient, moving slowly but surely toward the corner where Decca had been. Now the smoke was so thick it was impossible to tell where she had gone.

A panicked voice panted by his ear. "Wherever you're going, take me with you."

"Swanny, what are you doing?" Obi-Wan asked,

whirling his lightsaber to deflect a sudden barrage of blaster fire. "Stay by the band platform, you'll be safe there."

"Are you kidding? There *is* no band platform. Some Phlog stepped on it on the way to Striker's gang."

"We're sunk," Rorq said, suddenly appearing as he crawled up to Obi-Wan. "You've got to get us out of here."

Obi-Wan looked down at them, exasperated. The Force surged, and he quickly whirled around to slice an electrojabber in half, held by a Decca gang member who had mistaken him for an enemy.

He had to get to those datapads. He couldn't do that and protect Swanny and Rorq.

Obi-Wan leaped closer to Swanny, protecting him from a sudden barrage of fire from a repeating blaster. The fire was fast and furious. Obi-Wan had to twirl his lightsaber in a continuous motion. He called out to the Force, using it to slow down time so that he could see each individual blaster shot. Where was Anakin?

As if his thought had conjured him, Anakin appeared through the smoke. His lightsaber held high and constantly moving, he was leaping toward the repeating blaster, which some enterprising members of Striker's gang had set up against the wall.

Anakin hit the repeating blaster with both feet, using the split second between the blasts to make his strike. The blaster flew off its supports. Anakin came down, slicing the weapon in two.

Then he snaked his way back to Obi-Wan.

"Get Swanny and Rorq to safety," Obi-Wan shouted above the din. "I'm going to get to those records. As soon as they're safe, follow me." There was no time to come up with another plan. The smoke rolled toward him, and he plunged into it.

Instantly his eyes began to tear again, and he felt the smoke in his lungs, making his breathing difficult. He fought his way forward. Even in this smoke, it would be hard to hide a Hutt.

He had to step over the bodies of the dead and wounded. Obi-Wan tasted smoke and death in his mouth. He felt tiredness seep into his bones. Greed had that effect on him. He could better understand the Mawans, who had fought for ideas, than those who worked for the crimelords. Stamping out greed was impossible; controlling it was a never-ending task. His job would never be finished. In the middle of a battle such as this, a great tide of weariness could wash over him at the thought.

His battle mind had slipped. That wasn't good. Obi-Wan wrenched back his concentration. Suddenly the bank of datapads burst into flame. They had been hit by a grenade.

Obi-Wan stopped to consider what to do next. But he didn't have time to change his direction. A percussive force almost blasted him off his feet. The floor rose to meet him and he fell on one knee, his ears ringing. The size of the blast told him that it had been caused by a thermal detonator. More smoke filled the air, and he could hear screams and cries.

He leaped to avoid a sudden stab with a stun baton. His assailant disappeared into the smoke as quickly as he had appeared.

Obi-Wan decided to find Decca. If he followed her, he might discover her exit strategy and her backup plans. Perhaps she would lead him to another hideout. He reached the end of the substation at last. He could just glimpse Decca lowering her bulk into a specially designed speeder, wider and larger than normal. The pilot jammed its throttle forward, and it sped down the back tunnel.

He had missed the chance to follow her by seconds. There was no other speeder in the tunnel to take.

Obi-Wan turned. The smoke was clearing. He saw the gang members lying on the floor, or sitting, their heads in their hands. Some who could still run had taken off after the retreating members of Striker's gang.

Swanny was holding out a hand, helping Rorq to rise. They had taken cover behind a garbage bin.

Obi-Wan scanned the crowd. Where was Anakin?

He hurried over to Swanny and Rorq. "Did Anakin follow the others?"

Swanny shook his head. "I don't know, I didn't see. He pushed us back here just before something very big exploded."

The thermal detonator. What if Anakin had been close to it?

Something lay on the floor nearby. Obi-Wan felt a terrible dread steal over him. Slowly, he walked forward and crouched down by the object.

He picked it up and ran his fingers over it. The hilt was caked with dust and one deep scar now marred the finish.

It was Anakin's lightsaber.

CHAPTER SEVEN

At least I'm alive, Anakin thought. *I may be stupid, but I'm alive.*

It was a very un-Jedi thought. Jedi did not berate themselves. Anakin didn't care. He felt stupid and careless. He tried to rearrange himself within the garbage container he found himself in, but there was no room, and whenever he moved, his shoulder sent out a scream of protest. He wasn't hurt badly. He had landed on his shoulder when the thermal detonator hit. He had seen it but not soon enough. It had exploded, and he'd been hit.

And dropped his lightsaber. Something a Jedi was never, ever supposed to do.

Now he was being brought somewhere. He had been dazed from the thermal detonator, picked up like a sack of onions, and dropped into a container on top of a pile of greasy bones from the feast. His assailant had ripped his utility belt off his tunic, so he'd lost his comlink, too. He had been banged down the tunnel, been thrown into a vehicle, and now was careening . . . somewhere.

He couldn't wait to hear what his Master would say about this one.

Things were bad enough with Obi-Wan. What would happen when he found out that Anakin had lost his lightsaber and been captured?

Anakin pictured the exchange.

I saw the thermal detonator too late, Master. It was a surprise.

There are no surprises when the Force is with you, my young Padawan.

Anakin grimaced. He couldn't wait for that one. If he ever got out of here.

He moved his fingers along the container. It was a standard-issue garbage bin. The lid was hinged and had a simple lock. If he could manage to get on his back, he might be able to kick the lid with enough power to shatter the lock.

He could try it. He was on fire to get out of this stinking prison. But thanks to Obi-Wan, he had learned how to wait.

He was almost certain that he'd been captured by Striker's gang. Without his lightsaber, he might not be taken for a Jedi. Perhaps he was one of many prisoners. He guessed that he would be taken to Striker's hideout. He could bide his time and observe. They were here to gather information, after all. Maybe he could discover something valuable about Striker, something they could use.

So maybe the best thing he could do was lie here and wait to be released.

As he had that thought, Anakin felt the speeder slow. It stopped, and the container was grabbed roughly, then dropped. Anakin had braced himself, but he banged his head on the side. Patience was hard to find now, with a smarting head, but he reached for it, calming himself for whatever lay ahead.

The container lid was yanked open. Rough hands reached in. Anakin let his body go slack. He was grabbed and slung over someone's shoulder, then dumped on the ground.

Anakin looked up into cruel yellow eyes.

"There's your welcome, slug." A giant Imbat smiled down at him with mossy teeth. Then he reached for his utility belt, where a pair of stun cuffs dangled. They looked like delicate bracelets in his huge hand. He slapped them on to Anakin. Then with a grunt, he simply turned and walked off.

Anakin rose unsteadily to his feet. His shoulder still

ached, and he could feel a lump rising on the side of his forehead near his left eye.

Around him, activity swirled, but no one paid him any attention. He was free to wander, but the stun cuffs guaranteed he would not be able to wander far. From what he could tell, he was the only prisoner.

Anakin did what he knew Obi-Wan would want him to do. He observed.

The substation was even larger than the one Decca had used. Banks of monitoring equipment, now unused, ran along one wall. Benches and chairs had been ripped from their floor supports and were piled in a corner. A weapons rack held an impressive array of small arms.

The gang members were busy and didn't even glance at him. Some were checking and cleaning weapons. Others sat at improvised computer stations, entering information. Others manned comm units. Everyone seemed to have a job. Compared to the slipshod air of Feeana's operation and the chaos and suppressed violence of Decca's, this seemed like a professional operation.

Which told him that of all three criminals, Striker was the one to worry about.

Anakin had no idea where he was. How would Obi-Wan ever be able to find him?

But he didn't want Obi-Wan to find him. Not until he

had a chance to learn something. It would redeem him in his Master's eyes. Maybe he could discover something important and then escape.

Anakin drifted closer to the computer banks. He focused his attention on the fingers of a man entering information. He tapped into the Force to help him. He felt time slow down, and he tried to put words together from the letters the man was entering.

B I O . . . he missed several letters, someone walking by . . . P O N

T O X

Frustrated, Anakin leaned forward to see. A huge hand suddenly landed on his sore shoulder, sending a fresh jolt of pain through his body. "The boss wants to see you."

Without checking to make sure that he was following, the Imbat loped across the space. He accessed a durasteel door that led to a room off the main substation. He waited for it to open, then shoved Anakin inside. The door slid shut behind him.

The room was almost empty except for a bare table and one chair. The man standing in front of him was smiling and holding out his hands. "Forgive my manner of bringing you, my friend. I was impatient to see you."

Anakin felt shock ripple through him.

It was their greatest enemy, Granta Omega.

CHAPTER EIGHT

"You want us to bring you to Striker's hideout?" Swanny asked. "But no one knows where that is."

"You said you knew where everyone was, and everything that went on," Obi-Wan said.

"A slight exaggeration can often seal a deal," Swanny said. "Note the word 'hideout,' however. That implies that something is hidden, doesn't it?"

"Then we're just going to have to find it," Obi-Wan said.

"We?" Rorq asked. "What do we have to do with it?"

"Anakin came close to that thermal detonator because of the two of you," Obi-Wan said. "He saved your lives."

"And we're sure he wouldn't want us to lose them, after all the trouble he went to," Rorq said earnestly.

"Look, Master Obi," Swanny said. "The reason Striker is so effective is because nobody knows anything about him. They don't know where he came from. They don't know his name. They don't know where he lives. They don't know when he'll strike again. There are kilometers and kilometers of tunnels, some of them half finished, and empty substations on the perimeters. He could be anywhere. And it's not like we ever wanted to look very hard."

"Then we'll smoke him out," Obi-Wan said.

"I think I've had enough smoke for one night," Swanny said, rubbing his fingers along his smoke-blackened face.

"Not real smoke," Obi-Wan said. "I mean provoke him so that he'll come out into the open."

"Provoke him?" Rorq moaned. "That doesn't sound good."

Obi-Wan was feeling on the edge of his patience. He should have stayed with Anakin when they were under attack. Now he did not know if Anakin was badly wounded or worse.

He remembered feeling so angry on Andara. *I thought you'd be proud of me,* Anakin had said. And he had wanted to reply that he was proud, that Anakin's progress astonished him, that there was so much about Anakin that he admired. Instead he had held his tongue, thinking there would be a better time. He did not want to praise Anakin when his apprentice had made such an error.

But maybe he should have. That better time had not arrived.

"Where is Striker most vulnerable?" he asked Swanny.

"I have no idea," Swanny said. "Nowhere, if I had to guess. He's got personal guards that surround him at all times. Plus surveillance, weapons, assassins, a huge army . . . can I stop now?"

Obi-Wan's comlink signaled. He snatched it up eagerly.

"Speak with you, I must," Yaddle said. "At the airlift, meet we will."

"Of course," Obi-Wan said. "But I was just about to contact you. Anakin is missing. I think Striker has taken him."

Yaddle hesitated for only a beat. He could feel her concern. Then she said slowly, "Your problem, my problem — fix each other, they might."

Swanny and Rorq seemed relieved at the diversion. They were happy to lead him to the airlift.

Yaddle stepped off the airlift with the graceful, gliding step that never seemed to abandon her, even when she was tired or impatient.

"In addition to the mainframe substation of the power grid, taken over another crucial station, Striker has," she said. "Substation 32, a central relay station. Crucial it is as a network point for restarting the grid."

Swanny nodded. "That's right. He can override the power surge you need for start-up from that substation."

"Retake it, we must," Yaddle confirmed.

"I was looking for a way to provoke Striker," Obi-Wan said.

"That will do it," Swanny muttered. "He just got that substation back from Decca tonight. I imagine he feels pretty good about it."

"If we attack the substation, he'll have to send reinforcements," Obi-Wan said to Yaddle. "We can tail them back to the hideout."

"Can I say something here?" Swanny asked. "Taking the substation is impossible. Just wanted to mention that."

"What do you mean?" Obi-Wan asked.

"He has his best men protecting the power grid," Swanny said. "His most explosive weapons. I've seen the Jedi in action and it's a sweet sight, don't get me wrong. But can two Jedi go up against grenade launchers and missile tubes?"

Obi-Wan exchanged a glance with Yaddle.

"There's only one entrance to substation 32," Swanny went on. "It's the only way in. And you won't go more than two meters before you're blasted to pieces."

"I guess that's that, then," Rorq said. "There's no other way."

Yaddle smiled. Obi-Wan turned to Swanny and Rorq.

"For the Jedi, there is always another way," he said.

CHAPTER NINE

Don't let him see your surprise. Don't give him even a flicker of satisfaction.

"Oh, come on, Anakin," Granta Omega said. "You're surprised. Admit it. And maybe just a little bit pleased?" Omega smiled at him. Anakin was always mystified by his charm. He had liked him, once. Before he'd tried to kill Obi-Wan. Before it was clear that the dark side dominated his acts.

Granta Omega was out to lure a Sith into the open. He was not Force-sensitive, but he wanted to be close to the Force. He wanted to understand the source of such power. He would do anything to attract the one Sith he knew was at large in the galaxy. He was enormously wealthy, and would use anyone or anything to get what he wanted. Even the Jedi.

"I wouldn't say pleased," Anakin replied. "And I wouldn't say surprised. I'd say very unhappy."

Omega cocked his head and regarded Anakin. "I'm sorry to hear that. But I know that soon you'll understand why we keep running into each other. You are strong in the Force. Stronger than any Jedi. Stronger than your Master — and he knows it. I'm still interested in the Sith, but I'm becoming even more interested in you."

"The feeling isn't mutual."

Omega strolled around the empty room. He was what was known as a "void," a being who could neutralize his appearance and aura so completely that those who met him could not recall what he looked like. To Anakin, he'd seemed different each time they'd met. The first time he'd seen him, he'd appeared to be a weary bounty hunter. Anakin had also spent time with him when Omega was posing as a scientist named Tic Verdun. He'd had a haphazard, nervous manner then, and friendly brown eyes.

Now Anakin had the feeling he was seeing the real Granta Omega. His hair was dark and flowed to his shoulders. His eyes were a dark, deep blue, not brown as they'd appeared before. His body was slim but strong. And he looked younger, too, perhaps even younger than Obi-Wan.

"At least be impressed at how I've forgiven you," Omega said. "You notice I don't hold a grudge. You and your Master killed a good deal for me last time we met. I was close to cornering the market on bacta. I would have made a fortune. Instead I almost drowned in a tidal wave. Then I was forced to erase all my secret financial records. No hard feelings, though."

"On your side, maybe," Anakin said.

"As I was saying, that little adventure cost me. I had to make it up somehow. Planets like Mawan are made for beings like me. We can set up operations without too much interference. There's no one to bribe, no one to fight. We just grab our piece. I already had some business interests here, so it was just a matter of coming myself and devoting all my effort to it. I've made up what I lost in just a few months."

"Am I supposed to say congratulations now?" Anakin asked.

Omega sighed. "Still a Jedi," he said. "Moons and stars, you can be boring. Your Master's influence, no doubt." He leaned against the table. "Can't you relax? Not all Jedi are as rigid as your Master."

"How would you know?"

"Some are interested in investigating deep in the archives and finding that the Jedi know more about the dark side than they care to reveal. They don't waste their time meditating on favorite rocks in the Room of the Thousand Fountains or sneaking into the Council Receiving Room to watch the Senatorial starships dock in the restricted space lane."

"How do you know those things?" Anakin asked, startled. Only Jedi knew those things. They weren't important, but they were things that Padawans did.

"Maybe I know more about the Jedi than you," Omega said in a teasing tone. "Jealous?"

He laughed at the expression on Anakin's face. "You look worried. And angry. Didn't I suggest that you relax? You'd think you'd just gotten a reprimand from Rei Soffran."

Rei Soffran was a revered Jedi Master and a teacher of the intermediate students. He was legendary at the Temple for his tough lectures. When you were called to Rei Soffran's chamber, you knew your faults would be dissected and you'd be carved up like a roasted doisey bird.

But how did Omega know that?

Omega swung himself up on the table. He sat on the edge and faced Anakin, swinging his legs like a young boy. "Oh, come on, Anakin. You don't need Obi-Wan. You don't need the Council. Haven't you figured that out yet?"

Anakin thought of his last mission on Andara. He

had infiltrated a group of students who acted as a secret squad, hiring themselves out on missions throughout the galaxy. They chose what they wanted to do. They answered to no one but themselves. Before it all fell apart, he had admired them and maybe envied them. It had felt like freedom. It had made him think what he would be like without having a Master or the Council to tell him what to do. He had shoved those thoughts deep into his mind, like a dirty tunic in his utility bag.

Something must have changed in his face, for Omega's eyes gleamed, becoming a sharp, clear blue. "You *have* figured that out." He continued to study him. "But you can't face it."

Anakin shook his head. "That's not true."

Omega laughed. "I thought Jedi weren't supposed to lie. You've got one foot on the dark path, Anakin. Are you sure you are meant to be a Jedi?"

"It's all I've ever wanted," Anakin said. The words came out without him wanting them to. They were in his head, as they always were.

"Yes, you were a special case," Omega said. "I've heard the story. Chosen as a young boy. You were a slave, so of course you dreamed of a better life, a life you thought of as free. Welcome to reality, Anakin. Are you free?" Omega snorted. "If I held on to my dreams as a young boy, I'd be repairing starships for a living. I used to think that was exciting. How can you be so sure that your dream was the right one?"

"The dream is real because I am living it," Anakin said.

"The dream," Omega said softly, "was for opportunity and freedom and adventure. That is not the same thing. You began as a slave. Of course you dreamed of freedom. But you are not a boy now. You must know that the only thing that buys freedom in this life is wealth. I have it. I can give you more freedom than the Jedi can."

Anakin shook his head. "I don't want your brand of freedom."

"Why not? I can do anything I want. Let me tell you, power is a good thing to have. It's even fun. *You* could do anything you want. With my help, you could raise an army. You could return to the miserable planet of your birth and free your mother. Isn't that your deepest wish? Why are the Jedi holding you back from it?"

Startled, Anakin remembered his vision. He had touched the cuffs on Shmi's hands and they had fallen to the floor. It hadn't been a vision of what would happen, he realized suddenly. It had been a vision of what could be.

What could be . . .

The thought flared up, searing him with promise. He thought of how he'd felt in the dream. So powerful, so sure. Closing his hands over the remembered texture of Shmi's skin, seeing the light in her eyes when she saw him.

"Yes, Anakin Skywalker," Omega said softly. "I can give you the means to do it. We could leave here tomorrow if that's what you wished."

"No," Anakin said. *I am not listening to this. I am not hearing this.*

Omega pushed himself off the table. Anakin heard the slap of his boots on the floor, but he didn't look at his face. "Well, think about it. You don't have to leave the Jedi forever. You could give me a trial run. See how you like *real* freedom. You can always return to the Jedi. They're pretty desperate these days. They'll take you back."

"I will never give you anything," Anakin said.

"How about a deal? Something I want for something you want? I know the Jedi want me off-planet. I'm not sure if I'm ready to go, but if the Senate is going to get tangled up in Mawan politics, I'd be a fool to stay. Nevertheless, I have some demands. If you'll contact Yaddle and get her to come to a meeting here, I'll guarantee her safety."

"Who will guarantee yours?" Anakin shot back.

Omega chuckled. "You will. The fact that I'm holding a Jedi means that whoever is in charge up there won't send an army after me to 'negotiate.' I may be somewhat greedy, but I'm practical. I'm willing to move my operation. But Yaddle is the only one who can authorize my conditions. Set up the meeting. Then, while I make preparations to depart, you can decide whether you want to come with me."

"I don't have to make a decision. I know what I am. I know what I want."

Omega sighed. "You Jedi. Always so resolute." He shuddered. "All that self-righteousness gives me the spooks. Let me know if you'll set up the meeting. I'll arrange to bring your comlink to you."

He accessed the door and strode out into the busy substation. Anakin turned and watched him move across the room. He noticed how Omega quickly checked and conferred with his assistants as he walked. He made decisions quickly and moved on. The room hummed with activity. For the first time he saw how this man had amassed such a fortune.

How did Omega know such things about the Temple? Had he corrupted a Jedi? Had he infiltrated the Temple? Such things were unthinkable, but there had to be an explanation.

Omega's invitation for him to join his operation was

laughable. Yet it had brought the vision freshly into his mind, and Anakin still felt the ache of it.

We could leave here tomorrow. . . .

He could see her again. He could free her, and make sure she was well and safe. And then he could return to the Jedi. Omega said he could do that.

But the Jedi would not take him back if he did such a thing. Anakin knew that. Most likely Omega did, too. His offer was hollow at the core.

But was there truth there, too? Were the Jedi holding him back from his deepest wish?

And was he strong enough to face the answer?

CHAPTER TEN

Yaddle looked around the tunnel with distaste. "Too much time underground, I have spent," she murmured lightly. "Glad I will be to see the sky again."

Obi-Wan smiled at her humorous tone, but he knew there was truth behind Yaddle's words. He remembered the words from Anakin's vision: *The One Below remains below.* Yoda had interpreted it as a warning, and Obi-Wan agreed. Now Yaddle was belowground. What if the attack on the substation failed and something happened to Yaddle?

"I can handle this," he told her. "You should go back."

Yaddle shook her head at him. "Know what you are thinking, I do, Obi-Wan. Worried about your Padawan's vision, I am not. Think you that I should run away?"

"That's not what I meant, Master Yaddle," Obi-Wan said respectfully. "I was just suggesting that —"

"That run away I should," Yaddle interrupted. "Wasting time, we are."

Obi-Wan had been corrected, and he accepted Yaddle's rebuke. If he had been in her position, he would not have retreated, either. He turned to Swanny. "Didn't you tell me that you can boost the grid from another source, but only if the central relay substation is destroyed?"

"Right. Substation 32. That's my point," Swanny said patiently. "You might recall that I told you if you blow up the relay equipment, the whole power grid might blow. And that's one sweet ka-boom. Kiss your lightsaber good-bye."

Obi-Wan turned back to Yaddle. "If we hit substation 32, can your experts boost the grid right afterward? We can't give Striker a chance to hit back."

"Find out, we will." Yaddle immediately got out her comlink.

Swanny looked at Obi-Wan curiously. "I don't get it. How can two Jedi render an entire substation inoperable?"

"Well, we'll need a hand," Obi-Wan said. "That's where you come in."

"Me? You know I'd love to help, but I think you've seen my cowardice in action," Swanny said.

"You won't have to go near the substation," Obi-Wan assured him.

Yaddle got off the comlink and nodded. "Do it, they can. Yet crucial, timing is. Destroy the relay substation we must within the hour. Impatient, Feeana is. Need her we do to patrol the city. Trust us, the Mawan citizens must. If we promise them that control of the power grid and the backing of Feeana and her gang will hold the city, aboveground they will come." Yaddle paused. "An idea you have, Master Kenobi."

It was a statement, not a question.

"We can't blow it up," Obi-Wan said. "But we could drown it." He turned to Swanny. "Can you flood the substation from the wastewater pipes without getting inside the station? You said you knew every pipe belowground."

Swanny thought for a full minute while Obi-Wan tried not to show his impatience. "There's a small wash-up area in the substation for the workers," he said finally. "If I divert the wastewater from tank 102C and gush it through system A-9 with enough force, it could conceivably break through a pipe joint — the pipes going into substation 32 are part of the old system, so they're not in great shape — and then we'd have a pretty major flood in a matter of minutes. It would take me more than an hour to get there and figure out what circuits I need to use."

"You have forty minutes," Obi-Wan said. "We'd better get started."

Swanny had been right about the firepower. As Obi-Wan and Yaddle skirted the substation's perimeter, he could see two grenade mortars guarding the entrance. The operators sat on repulsorlift platforms, and the Jedi could see that the targeting computers were engaged. Attack droids stood in ready formation.

"We could use a diversion," Obi-Wan murmured to Yaddle as they hid behind a utility box.

"Accomplish this we must, if the Provisional Committee is going to be successful," Yaddle said. "The longer it takes, the more things can go wrong."

"Look," Obi-Wan said, pointing at a stream of water underneath the double durasteel doors of the substation. "Swanny must have been effective. The flood has begun."

Yaddle opened her comlink to signal the power grid team that Euraana had arranged to stand by.

Up on their repulsorlift platforms, the guards didn't notice the water streaming out from underneath the crack in the durasteel doors. Their gazes continued to rest on the targeting computers that would show them attacking beings or airborne weapons.

"When it gets deep enough to endanger the equipment, the alarm should sound," Obi-Wan murmured. "I'm betting the operators will leave their grenade mortars and let the droids guard the entrance. They'll call for reinforcements."

"One problem, there is," Yaddle said. "Burst open, the doors might."

"And that would release the flood into the tunnel." Obi-Wan nodded. "In which case, the equipment might keep functioning." He thought for a moment. "Can you use the Force to hold the doors?"

Yaddle nodded.

The water was now streaming down the tunnel and lapping at their boots. Because of the downward slope, it ran out from underneath the door. They could see that the water inside was rising, since the water was now leaking out of the seam between the double doors. The pressure of the water was causing the doors to vibrate from the strain.

Obi-Wan felt the Force surround them as Yaddle gathered it around her. The doors and the water stopped moving. It began to collect around the wheels of the grenade mortars and the legs of the droids.

They watched as the water deepened, held back by

the Force. Soon it was lapping at the repulsorlift plat-forms, but the guards still did not notice, intent on their computers.

Suddenly a light flashed red over the doors. The alarm began to beep insistently. The two operators sat up in their chairs and swiveled to check behind them. They saw the water.

"What's going on?" one of them shouted.

The other spoke into a comlink. "They're sending re-inforcements. Just stay calm."

"I am calm!" the second guard shouted. "I just can't swim!"

The other guard began to enter a code into a hand-held sensor.

"They'd better boost the grid now," Obi-Wan said.

Yaddle listened intently to the comlink.

"Bypassed the station, they have," she told Obi-Wan. "Wait we must to see if the power surge will re-store the grid. . . ."

Suddenly the attack droids snapped into formation, splashing in the water.

"They must have engaged a life-form sensor sweep," Obi-Wan said.

"A few minutes more, they need."

"We just ran out of time." Obi-Wan activated his lightsaber. "Let's go."

He charged out into the tunnel, moving quickly through the water and heading straight for the mortar operators. They saw the Jedi charging and scrambled to jump back on their mortar platforms. Yaddle released her hold on the doors, which burst open, releasing a wave of water. Obi-Wan was prepared, but the power of the water almost knocked him down. He reached out a hand, using the Force to push one guard off his feet. His head hit the durasteel doors and he slumped to the floor as the water flowed down the tunnel.

Right behind Obi-Wan, Yaddle took out an attack droid with a flick of her lightsaber while she sent the other guard flying against the tunnel wall. The last guard took one look at the Jedi charging toward him with a lightsaber and took off, splashing down the tunnel.

Attack droids cannot be intimidated, however. The line wheeled toward the Jedi. Obi-Wan had never fought beside Yaddle before. She was all grace and flowing movement, her lightsaber a blur, the Force growing and charging the air around them until Obi-Wan could feel it humming in him and around him. Charged with Yaddle's energy, he sliced through four droids with one swift blow. The blaster fire was heavy but he had no problem deflecting it. It felt easy and natural with the Force so strong. Yaddle took out ten attack droids in what seemed like no time and then buried her lightsaber in the two grenade mortar controls. Within minutes, all of the droids were sizzling in the puddles of water.

"Reinforcements should be here soon," Obi-Wan said.

"Feel them near, I can," Yaddle said. She listened to the comlink and then nodded. "Success," she said to Obi-Wan. "Up, the power grid is, and in our hands. The city of Naatan is lit once more. Go now to the Mawans, I must. Time to return to their homes, it is."

Obi-Wan nodded. "I'll wait for the reinforcements. They'll most likely return to brief Striker."

"As soon as I can return to help find Anakin I will," Yaddle said.

Yaddle moved down the tunnel quickly, her robe swinging. Obi-Wan stepped back behind the utility box and waited. The tramp of running feet announced the arrival of the reinforcements.

They took one look at the spreading water, the still-sizzling droid parts, and the absence of the guards. The superior officer activated his comlink and spoke into it. Then he signaled to the others.

"Nothing we can do here," the officer said.

"Aren't you going to search the tunnels?" another one asked.

"Do I look crazy? Back to headquarters."

They tramped off. After a moment, Obi-Wan emerged from behind the utility box and followed.

CHAPTER ELEVEN

He was grateful, at least, for the food. Anakin had considered rejecting the plate of vegetable turnovers with harima sauce, but what good would that do? He'd finished the plate and downed a carafe of water when suddenly Granta Omega strode out of his private room and the hideout exploded in movement.

He couldn't hear the orders Omega rapped out but suddenly everyone was busy. Computers were shut down. Bins were closed and locked. Weapons were gathered. Gravsleds appeared and gang members began loading them.

Obi-Wan, Anakin thought. He smiled.

Within minutes, the substation was cleared.

Still cuffed, Anakin was hustled into a speeder with the same Imbat guard. He zoomed down the tunnel at a fast clip. Anakin kept his mind focused so he could remember the many turns.

At last they arrived at their destination, a smaller space that had once been a refueling center. Anakin was tossed out of the speeder by the Imbat, but this time he was able to land on his feet. He watched while the gang members busily began to set up the hideout again. He could see that they had done this many times.

Granta Omega strode toward him, his boot heels clicking on the floor. He looked grim. "It's time to contact Yaddle."

"As long as I can tell her who you are and I can speak freely." He had nothing to lose by contacting Yaddle. He had complete confidence that she'd be able to handle Granta Omega. And Yaddle would be able to tell Obi-Wan that he was still alive.

Omega waved a hand. "Of course. I'm not trying to trick you, Anakin. I'm a businessman. I want to make a deal."

"I'll need my comlink."

Omega tossed it to him.

"As long as I have it, I'd like to contact my Master, too," Anakin said. It was worth a try.

"Do you think he's worried about you?" Omega barked a laugh. "What you don't know about your Master could fill your precious archives. Kenobi doesn't have a heart. Beings are just a means to get what he needs to be — the great Jedi in his own mind."

Anakin suddenly grasped a feeling that had floated in his mind, something he could not put words to. Now it formed into a belief.

"This is personal for you, isn't it?" he accused Omega. "You hate Obi-Wan."

Omega flushed. "No calls to your Master. I deal with Yaddle only. I only have so much hospitality to offer."

Anakin contacted Yaddle. There was nothing else to do. He quickly explained that Striker was actually Granta Omega, and that he was his prisoner, which was hard to get out. He still felt ashamed that he had allowed himself to be captured.

"Omega has requested a meeting," he finished. "He will only meet with you."

"Hold you hostage, he did not need to do," Yaddle said. "Talk to him, I would have done, if he had asked."

"I guess he feels he needs some insurance that you will come alone," Anakin said. "He's afraid that if he sets up a meeting he will be betrayed."

"I'm not afraid," Omega hissed to Anakin. "Just careful."

"I can't tell you where I am, because I'm not sure," Anakin said. "We just moved to a new hideout. And I don't know how sincere Omega is about making a deal. He says he is, but I don't trust him." Omega grinned at Anakin, not bothered in the least. "It is up to you to decide, Master Yaddle. All I ask is that you do not come because of me. I am fine here."

"So far," Omega said so that Yaddle could hear.

"Come, I will," Yaddle said. "But inform Obi-Wan first, I must."

"I have a list of coordinates," Omega said to Anakin. "I'll release them one at a time. If at any point it seems that Yaddle is not alone, I will disappear . . . with you."

"Understood," Yaddle said, after Anakin had conveyed this information.

Anakin clutched his comlink. He hoped they both had made the right decision. "May the Force be with you," he told Yaddle.

Omega rolled his eyes. "Oh, please," he said.

"Striker is Granta Omega?" Obi-Wan hissed into his comlink. He had concealed himself in the near-empty substation to watch the activity. The gang he had followed had come directly here, but it was obvious the main hideout had been moved. Now they were occupied in gathering up the last weapons and equipment and loading them onto speeders with cargo holds.

"Going to meet him, I am," Yaddle said.

"I'm coming with you."

"Best you do not," Yaddle said.

"He is my Padawan —"

"And trust me with his security you do not?"

Obi-Wan held the comlink away and sighed. He rested his head against the smooth surface of the tunnel wall. It was hard being matched up with an esteemed Jedi Master like Yaddle. He would not win any argument.

"Moved his hideout, Omega has. It would take us too long to find it. A shortcut, this is." Yaddle's voice softened slightly. "Watch out for him, I will, Obi-Wan. But need you I do, to help with the Mawans. Agreed they have to go aboveground. The exodus is proceeding. A Jedi presence is needed here."

Obi-Wan took a moment to accept this. It went against everything he wanted. He needed to see Anakin with his own eyes, to make sure he was safe and well. But Yaddle had told him that Anakin said he was fine, and his voice had sounded strong.

He needed to see Granta Omega, too. Anger rose in him, anger that made him want to put his fist through a wall. Anger he must learn to accept and release.

Omega had his Padawan. His most dangerous enemy had his most treasured companion. And instead of helping to release Anakin, Yaddle was asking him to shepherd complete strangers back to their homes.

It was that thought that helped him. He was a Jedi. The needs of strangers were most important. His own needs meant nothing in comparison to theirs. Obi-Wan repeated the words again in his mind, this time with the compassion and power that they warranted. He had to bring strangers safely to their homes.

"All right," he said to Yaddle. "But tell Omega that I will see him soon."

"A threat that is," Yaddle said sternly. "And so deliver it I will not."

Obi-Wan rested his head against the wall again.

"Unless I have to," Yaddle concluded.

Anakin stood, waiting for Yaddle. Omega was using tracking droids to make sure Yaddle came to each co-ordinate alone.

They were in one of the airlift tube stations, smaller than the one Anakin had used to come below only hours ago, though it felt like days. He guessed he was about twenty levels down, near the northeast quadrant of the tunnel system. If he had to find his way back to Obi-Wan, he might be able to.

"She's following my instructions," Omega said. "Smart."

"What did you expect?" Anakin said. "She's not afraid of you."

"Yes, I can always depend on Jedi arrogance," Omega said. "In an uncertain galaxy, it's so comforting to have one thing you can count on. Tell me, Anakin. Have you thought about what I said? I'll make the deal with Yaddle and we can go to Tatooine tonight. You could see your mother as early as tomorrow. I have a fast ship."

"I didn't need to think about what you said."

"Ah, but you did think about it, I can tell. This is your last chance. I hate to be dramatic, but . . ." Omega shrugged. "Choose."

"There is no choice," Anakin said.

"Too bad. Your loss. Mine too, that's the sad thing. Ah, the wee one approaches."

Yaddle came toward them, her robe swinging with the motion of her walk.

"Thank you for coming," Omega said courteously.

Yaddle studied Anakin for a moment. He saw her gaze rest on his stun cuffs, then move on. Her eyes met his, and he nodded to show her that he was all right.

"Understand I do that you have conditions, but willing you are to leave Mawan," Yaddle said.

"Willing? Hardly. I have a good thing here," Omega said.

"Choose to leave you may not, but warn you I must,"

Yaddle said. "Hunted you will be, by Senate security forces. By midday, under our control Naatan will be."

"Impressed with your speed I am," Omega said, mocking Yaddle.

Yaddle did not show anger or impatience, yet Anakin saw something flare in her eyes, something very much like defiance. "And wish he did for me to tell you, Obi-Wan will meet you soon."

Omega laughed. "I'm sure he did. I wish I could say I'm looking forward to it, but Kenobi puts me to sleep."

"Waiting to hear your conditions I am," Yaddle said.

"Let me start by telling you that I am in possession of a highly illegal bioweapon."

Anakin felt his stomach twist. He remembered the fingers tapping out information. B I O P O N — Bioweapon! He should have put that together! And the next letters he'd glimpsed had been T O X . . .

"It is a simple device, really," Omega went on. "Beautifully simple. Basically a canister packed with a powerful explosive. But the canister is filled with di-hexalon gas. Are you familiar with it?"

"Toxic to life-forms, it is," Yaddle said. "Deadly."

"Good, then you know what we are dealing with. The canister has been loaded into this airlift tube. The det-onator is controlled by a remote device that is not on me, but I can transmit the order in seconds. I know you've been leading the Mawans back to their homes on the surface. That's Obi-Wan's job, isn't it? Pity they all will die."

"You targeted Obi-Wan?" Anakin asked, fury ticking beneath his words.

"No, your Master is just a bonus." Omega eyed Yaddle. "You should know by now that I have bigger ambitions."

Yaddle met his gaze. Anakin felt the Force stir. It seemed to rustle around his ankles, then move up his body, as if Yaddle was drawing it from the ground itself. He felt it like a physical sensation.

"Wish you do to kill a Council Member," Yaddle said.

"I'm afraid so," Omega said.

Anakin realized then that he was just a pawn in this struggle. Omega had used him. He had let himself be used. He had been so stupid!

"You must choose," Omega said. "The lives of the Mawans — or the life of Anakin Skywalker, the Chosen One."

"Or my own life," Yaddle said. "So many lives, you play with."

"That's my job. Those cuffs on Anakin's wrists are not stun cuffs," Omega said. "They carry enough of a charge to kill him."

Anakin looked down at the cuffs on his wrists. He had done this. He had been the bait to lure Yaddle here. Omega had lied. He still wanted to impress a Sith. And what better way than to kill a Jedi Council member?

"Your death will be painless, Master Yaddle," Omega said. "I'll give you that. I'm not interested in giving you pain. Anakin will bring the news back to Obi-Wan. It will soon be known around the galaxy."

"And the bioweapon?" Yaddle asked.

"That's my insurance that I will get off-planet," Omega said. "With my soldiers, with my equipment, with my wealth, with my records. But The One Below will remain below. I will seal your legend, Master Yaddle."

The One Below will remain below . . .

Omega would have revenge on Anakin as well. Anakin would have to live knowing he had caused Yaddle's death.

"So what do you —" Omega started.

The movement was so sudden and so fast that even Anakin couldn't track it. Yaddle's lightsaber was activated without him seeing her move so much as a finger. She used it in a surgical strike at his wrists. He did not have time to flinch, which was lucky, because she could easily have cut off his hands. Anakin felt only a flash of heat, as though he'd touched something hot and then pulled his hand away.

The cuffs clattered to the floor.

The cuffs, falling . . .

That was in his vision, too! But the cuffs hadn't been on Shmi. They had nothing to do with Shmi. Obi-Wan and Yoda had been right.

"Launch it!" Omega screamed, then turned to Yaddle and added, "You have just ensured the deaths of thousands."

Anakin realized in a flash that Omega must have had an open channel on his comlink. That had been an order. He heard the rush of air in the tube.

He only saw the flash of the hem of Yaddle's robe as she Force-jumped toward the airlift tube. She pressed the maximum eject button with the hilt of her lightsaber as she passed. She burst into the airlift tube and shot upward like a blast from a laser cannon.

Omega was too stunned to move. Anakin didn't hesitate. He jumped after Yaddle into the tube, pressing the maximum eject button as well.

The velocity was incredible. He shot upward to the surface so fast he lost his breath and his ears protested with a scream of pain. He shot out into a night sky that glittered with stars. The lights of the city were a blur as he passed them. He started to fall back down, the wind whistling past his ears. Only the Force saved him from an extremely bumpy landing. He called on it to slow his descent but still he landed hard, bending his knees and rolling with the impact.

He lay on his back, still dizzy, trying to catch his breath. Yaddle had not landed. He felt the Force so strongly it served to yank him to his feet. Again, it was like a physical presence to him, as though he could feel it on his skin and even in the roots of his hair.

Yaddle hung above him, above the tallest building of Naatan, the Force holding her temporarily aloft. She held a silver canister against her chest.

She was high above, but he heard her voice clearly. It was in his head, he realized.

If you lose your anger, find you it will. Embrace it and disappear it will. Chosen, you may be. But for what? Your question to answer, it is.

He barely registered her words. A terrible certainty was growing. And then everything was suddenly clear to Anakin, as clear as the hard-edged stars. He realized what Yaddle was about to do.

"No!" he shouted. But he could already feel it. Yaddle was drawing in the great net of the Force she had created, drawing it around her so tightly and fiercely and strongly that Anakin fell to his knees. He had never felt the Force move like this. He couldn't speak or move.

From far below, Granta detonated the explosives.

Anakin heard a sharp pop, nothing more. The Force grew until Anakin was dazzled. Instead of exploding, the canister imploded, and Yaddle drew the toxic gas and the explosive power in, absorbing it into her body.

Then she simply disappeared. A shower of light particles swirled, hung in the air, then evaporated.

Anakin's face was wet. Tears flowed and he did not feel them. The night sky was empty, and Jedi Master Yaddle was dead.

CHAPTER TWELVE

Anakin sat, staring at the ground. He did not feel time passing. Somewhere in his mind he knew he should find a comlink, find a way to contact Obi-Wan, but the thought was distant and he did not pursue it.

Yaddle was dead. He knew it, but he couldn't grasp it. A member of the Jedi Council, a wise being so practiced in the Force that she was a legend. A being whose strength and wisdom the Jedi needed in these times. She had sacrificed herself for him. Because he had seen a thermal detonator too late. Because he had been captured. Because he had been tricked. A chain of events had brought him to this moment. At any time he could have changed his course. Instead he had blundered on.

She had saved him first, then gone after the bomb.

Anakin puzzled over that. She had risked thousands of lives for his. Why?

Chosen, you may be. But for what? Your question to answer, it is.

Was that why she had saved him?

If that was the reason, he could not bear the responsibility. Her death was his fault.

A pair of dusty, muddy boots appeared. Obi-Wan crouched down.

"Something terrible has happened," he said. "I felt the Force surge, and then retreat, like a vacuum. Tell me."

"Master Yaddle is dead," Anakin said, his voice muffled.

Obi-Wan breathed in, absorbing his shock. "How?"

Anakin told him the story in a neutral tone. If he added his feelings to the telling, he would not be able to finish.

Obi-Wan was silent for long moments. He sat back on his heels and looked up at the sky.

"She went below for me," Anakin said. "She saved me first. If I hadn't been captured . . ."

"Stop." It was Obi-Wan's sternest tone. "Jedi do not go down the path of 'ifs.' You know that, Anakin. You choose in each moment what your next step will be. You do not look back in judgment."

Obi-Wan stood. "Yaddle made the only choice she could, and she made it freely."

Obi-Wan reached down. Anakin's lightsaber was in his hand.

"We will mourn her, but not now. Now it is time to be a Jedi."

Anakin took the lightsaber. He rose and tucked it into his belt. His Master's words should have made Anakin feel better, but they hadn't. They had almost seemed automatic, as though Obi-Wan didn't really mean them.

Even Obi-Wan thought Anakin was responsible for Yaddle's death.

Sorrow and guilt filled him up so far he felt he was drowning.

And then there was an explosion of light and sorrow . . . He had lost, in fact, everyone he loved, including Obi-Wan.

The vision had been right.

CHAPTER THIRTEEN

Obi-Wan contacted Yoda on the emergency channel. He hated having to be the one to break the news. He would bring Yoda great pain. He felt the pain himself, in the way his body moved like lead. He had barely been able to summon up the right words to say to Anakin, and he knew his words had not reached him.

All he could think of was Yaddle. She had been part of his life from his earliest memory. She had taken special delight in the young Jedi students. She had turned a blind eye to their pranks. She had hidden sweets in their pockets. Her touch on the top of his head had felt like the most comforting thing in the world.

And then he had grown, and things at the Temple had become more serious. There were hard lessons to learn. Yaddle had been there, in a different way. There had been so many times when he had knocked respectfully on her door with a problem he did not want to trouble Yoda with. Obi-Wan realized how exceptional it was that a member of the Jedi Council had allowed herself to be so available to every student. Obi-Wan had not been the only one to seek her counsel, to look for comfort there.

He had lost something so precious. It had been a part of his life for so long he hadn't seen it clearly. Yaddle had just been there, with her quiet wisdom. It was almost as bad as losing Yoda would be.

He gave Yoda the details quickly, knowing he would want to hear everything.

Yoda's voice was liquid with sorrow. "Felt the Force move, I did. Know I did that she was gone. Prepared my transport for Mawan, I already have. Her work, we must carry on. May the Force be with us."

They hadn't slept since Coruscant, but there was no time for sleep. With Yaddle's death, the fragile coalition she had formed threatened to fall apart. News of the bioweapon had spread, and the Mawans were close to panic. If Granta Omega had a weapon that devastating, who could say that he did not have another?

Within hours, the Senate went back on their pledge to send a security force and sent word that they would await further developments. They would not commit an army to an unstable situation.

Anakin dropped his head in his hands at this news. "Isn't the instability the point? That's why we need them!"

Obi-Wan sighed. "Yes, but if the security force is beaten by crimelords, the Senators are afraid it will look bad for them. Their image is more important than Mawan's security."

"What can we do?" Anakin asked.

"That's the simple part. Present them with an easy win," Obi-Wan answered. "The hard part is setting that up. Granta Omega has become our biggest problem."

"He would be happy to hear that," Anakin said.

They sat in a small office in the makeshift command center the Senate Provisional Committee had set up. Now that the power grid was functioning, they could monitor the streets through a system of security cams set up around the city. Many had been smashed, but some were still functioning, enough to give them a sense of what was going on. The streets were eerily quiet. Criminal activity had either retreated into buildings or gone underground. The sun was just rising, penetrating the gray with a blush of pink. Obi-Wan wished he felt as hopeful as the scene painted.

Euraana Fall entered, her face pale with fatigue and worry. "Feeana Tala is close to deserting the city and pulling her patrols. She doesn't think we can hold the city against an attack by Omega."

"That means the city will be left without security," Anakin said.

"Which means everyone will retreat belowground again, and we'll be back where we started," Euraana said, lowering herself into a chair. She bent forward to lean her forehead against her clasped hands. She closed her eyes. "I'm hoarse from talking and reasoning. I don't know what else to do. I've been in communication with the Senate representative. He refuses to reconsider the decision to pull back the Senate security force."

"I will speak with him," Obi-Wan said. "And I'll handle Feeana as well. Let's go, Anakin." It seemed a great effort to haul himself out of his chair. Obi-Wan felt the fatigue deep in his bones. "We'll grab some food on the way," he said to Anakin, and saw the boy's face brighten slightly.

They headed to the café on the second level. Once it had served the many Mawans who had flocked to the hall for music and lectures, and its extensive stoves and cooling units spoke of the array of foods that had once been offered. Now the shelves were bare. At least there was hot tea and a tray of muja muffins.

Anakin picked one up. "Stale," he said, disappointed. "Why do the bad guys get all the good food?"

Obi-Wan held up his tea. "That's what dunking is for. Another Jedi lesson for you."

Anakin tried to smile. It was the first light moment they had exchanged since Yaddle's death. But a moment later, Anakin's face darkened again.

Something is very wrong, Obi-Wan thought. It wasn't just the aftermath of Yaddle's death. Why was it that whenever he needed to talk to his Padawan, circumstances got in the way? There was always a mission to complete, and then, these days, as soon as they were done, there was somewhere else important to go, another crucial battle to fight.

Across the empty tables Obi-Wan spied Feeana Tala, slumped over a mug of tea. This was a bit of luck. He could approach her informally. Sometimes that was better when you were trying to hold on to a deal. It would be easier to ensure the Senate's support if he could be sure Feeana would not fold.

Feeana looked as tired as Euraana had. She waved Obi-Wan off as he approached. "Go away."

Obi-Wan sat down, summoning up a cheerful smile.

He motioned Anakin to do the same. He dunked a piece of muffin into his tea. "Good morning to you, too."

"Don't bother with the pleasantries," Feeana said. "I know why you're here. You're going to tell me that my cooperation is essential in holding the city. You're going to say that as a Mawan I owe it to my home planet. You're going to say that if I take my gang and retreat below-ground that eventually I'll be imprisoned." She stirred her tea moodily. "I know all those things. But I've got my soldiers out on the streets, and there's not enough of them to hold the city against Striker — or Omega, as I hear his name is. What am I supposed to do? Send them to their deaths?"

"I would not ask you to continue patrolling the city if I thought that," Obi-Wan said. "I am not willing to sacrifice so many lives to get what we need."

"But Decca and Omega —"

"We can handle Decca and Omega."

She placed her spoon down carefully. "So you say. And yet a Jedi Master evaporated into dust particles just a few hours ago."

"Yaddle died in order to protect your soldiers and the people of Mawan," Obi-Wan said sharply. "That should tell you how far the Jedi are willing to go."

There was a short silence. Feeana sipped her tea

and made a face. "It's cold," she said. Then slowly, she nodded. "All right," she continued quietly. "I'll remain."

With Feeana's cooperation and the promise of Yoda's arrival, Obi-Wan was able to convince the Senate to aid Mawan. He found it difficult to keep his temper cool and speak reasonably. He wanted to shout at everyone that Yaddle had sacrificed herself for their peace and security, so the least they could do was follow through. He knew that grief was making him short-tempered. His heart was heavy, and he was angry, too, angry that Yaddle had to die.

These were emotions he could not carry with him, for they would drag him down. He had to absorb them and let them go. Yet he felt as though he was struggling against a rising tide.

Anakin said so little. He could not get up the energy to address his Padawan's need, either. And somewhere below, Granta Omega was biding his time, concocting his plan for revenge, and he would surely try to exploit Anakin's sadness for his own ends. Omega had already killed a member of the Jedi Council. That had been his great goal, and he had achieved it.

How could Obi-Wan get rid of his anger when he knew of Omega's satisfaction?

A silver streak in the sky told them that Yoda was arriving. They were on the lookout for it, and they hurried toward the landing site. The day had dawned gray and cold. A sudden dip in temperature had kept most beings inside. It was a lucky break. If Feeana's security patrols didn't have to worry about petty crime, it would be easier to keep them at their posts.

Yoda alighted from the cruiser. His gaze immediately went to Anakin.

"First, see it, I must."

Anakin nodded. He knew immediately what Master Yoda was asking. Yoda wanted to see the place where Yaddle had died.

For long moments, Yoda stood underneath the spot where Yaddle's life had ended. He leaned his head back as if to taste the air. He closed his eyes as if to feel the presence that still lingered. Obi-Wan imagined that he was saying a private, final good-bye to the friend he'd had for so long. He turned away, wanting to give Yoda the moment. Anakin's gaze rested on the ground.

At last Yoda turned. "Ready, I am," he said.

They headed back toward the command center. They found Swanny and Rorq waiting for them, sitting on the steps. They stood as the Jedi approached.

"Bad news," Swanny said. "Decca and Omega have settled their feud. They've formed an alliance."

"I was afraid of this," Obi-Wan said.

"It gets worse. Now Omega has access to Decca's fleet, and Decca has access to Omega's weapons. They are planning an assault on the city."

"We have no way to protect the city," Obi-Wan told Yoda. "All we have are security patrols."

"Then prevent the attack we must," Yoda said. "The strengths they have are transports and weaponry? Then strengths we must attack."

"I'm getting tired of saying that's impossible," Swanny said. "But this time, it really is. Decca just got a big shipment of fuel. It was part of the partnership deal — Omega supplied it. They just brought it below."

"A shipment of fuel," Obi-Wan murmured. "That might help us."

Swanny looked at him, incredulous. "I don't see how. But I have a feeling I will."

"Keep the information about the alliance quiet for now," Obi-Wan said. "If Feeana gets wind of this —"

"Uh, I think it might be too late," Rorq said. He pointed to the distance, where Feeana was striding toward them, an angry look on her face.

"They have formed an alliance!" she exclaimed as she walked up.

"We know," Obi-Wan said.

"And you are just standing here?" she demanded.

"A suggestion, you have for us?" Yoda asked mildly.

She noticed him for the first time. "Who's this?"

"Jedi Master Yoda," Obi-Wan said. "One of our most esteemed Masters."

"Whatever," Feeana said. "Maybe he can tell me what I should do when Omega and Decca attack my troops with transports and missile tubes?"

"Stop the attack before it starts, we will," Yoda said.

"How?" Feeana demanded. "If you expect me to co-operate, I need more to go on."

"Just trust us," Obi-Wan said. "We need you to patrol all the airlift tube exits. As soon as we have control belowground, we will contact you."

"I guess I have no choice," Feeana said.

"Choice, you always have," Yoda told her. "But the best one this is."

A struggle still on her face, Feeana strode away.

"Well, I guess we'll just say good-bye and good luck," Swanny said, beginning to head off. Obi-Wan caught him by his collar.

"Not so fast," he said. "You're coming with us."

CHAPTER FOURTEEN

Anakin was glad to go belowground. Being under the open sky where Yaddle had died had affected him. The sky had seemed to hang over him, pressing against his shoulder blades. Below in the tunnels, he felt safer.

Revenge was on his mind, and it frightened him. He hated Granta Omega, hated him with a burning rage that threatened to go out of control. He was grateful that Yoda had joined them. The presence of the great, perhaps the greatest, Jedi Master was as deep and huge as Anakin's rage. Surely it would keep his anger in check. He would look to his Master and Yoda for the control he needed.

He knew that Yoda and Obi-Wan also felt anger and grief. He saw it in their eyes, felt it in the air around them, noted it in the way they moved and spoke. Yet they were not deflected from their mission. He had watched in awe as they exchanged information. Their shared glances told him that they had both come up with the same plan, at the same time. Yoda was obviously grief-stricken, yet he had traveled here to finish a job that Yaddle had begun, and he would let nothing stand in his way, not even his own sorrow.

He had been so wrong, Anakin thought suddenly. On Andara, he had briefly imagined what it could be like to have no Master, no Council to answer to. But he needed the Council. He needed his Master. They showed him how far he had to go.

Their inner calm was something he desperately wanted. He would learn, he promised himself. On every mission he was brought up short and shown what he needed to concentrate on. But he would learn.

If I can get Obi-Wan's trust back.

Anakin felt as though he were drowning. Drowning in his guilt. Everything had changed for him now. Master Yaddle had died before his eyes, and it had marked him forever. He knew that as firmly as he knew his own name. As surely as he knew he would do anything now to be a Jedi Knight.

"Okay, here we are," Swanny said, standing in front of

a map of the wastewater transport system. "What do you have in mind? Are you going to flood the fuel depot?"

"We'd never get away with that," Obi-Wan said. "Too many people around. I had something else in mind." He pointed to the map. "Here's Decca's fuel depot. Where are the fuel storage tanks?"

Rorq pointed to a spot several levels above. "Here. The fuel is pumped into a big storage tank here, then into the individual tanks in the depot."

Obi-Wan turned to Swanny. "Is there anyplace where the wastewater pipes come close to the fueling pipes between storage and the depot?"

"Sure," Swanny said. "The pipes run this way and cross the wastewater pipes here." He stabbed at a spot on the map.

"Where is that?" Obi-Wan asked. "Is it in Omega's or Decca's territory?"

"No, it's close to where the Mawan tent city was," Swanny said. He whistled. "I think I'm getting this."

"Is it possible?" Obi-Wan asked.

"We'd have to cut through the pipes and do some hydro-welding," Swanny said. "But that's like a walk in the park for us."

"It's almost too simple," Rorq marveled.

Yoda nodded. "The best plan, the simple one is," he said.

Anakin saw what Yoda and Obi-Wan had already figured out on the surface. Decca's fleet would fuel in the depot. But if they could replace the fuel with wastewater before it reached the depot, she would fill her transports with water instead of fuel. That would immobilize them completely. Even if they pumped out the tanks, it would take them days to dry out. Any water in the fuel would cause problems with the engines. It was beautifully simple.

"We'll need to know if they start refueling, though," Swanny said. "If we're working on the pipes at the same time, we could end up hip-deep in fuel."

"We'll keep an eye on the fueling depot," Obi-Wan said. "Anakin will be sure to protect you while you work." Obi-Wan spoke to Anakin. "As soon as Swanny and Rorq are done, join us at the fuel depot."

Anakin nodded. He was glad to have a task, even if it was only guarding Swanny and Rorq.

They split up. Anakin followed Swanny and Rorq through the tunnels toward the designated spot. Swanny stopped at a utility shed that had a serious locking device wrapped around the door.

"We need tools," Swanny said. "We'll have to break into this. It could take a while. If I had a fusioncutter I could break in, but the fusioncutter is in the shed."

"Not a problem," Anakin said. He activated his

lightsaber and cut through the metal door in less than a second.

"I've got to stop underestimating you guys," Swanny said.

He and Rorq reached in and grabbed what they needed. Then they hurried on. They reached the designated spot and Swanny and Rorq began to work. Rorq opened a small door set into the tunnel wall. Behind it was a crawl space that was crisscrossed with pipes.

"You sure you know which is which?" Anakin asked.

"Do I ask you if you know your job?" Swanny asked.

"All the time."

"Oh. True. Well, trust me." With a grunt, Swanny closed the valve on a pipe, then began to cut through the metal with a macrofuser.

The minutes ticked by. Anakin shifted from one foot to another. His comlink signaled, and he answered it.

"Decca's crew has arrived. They're going to start fueling," Obi-Wan said. "How close are they to finishing?"

Anakin asked Swanny, who held up three fingers.

"Three minutes."

"Make it two," Obi-Wan said.

"Almost," Swanny said, fitting a short length of pipe between the two pipes they had been working on. "We just need to fuse" — he bent over with the macrofuser — "and seal . . ."

"Hurry," Obi-Wan said. "They've released the hoses."

". . . one more second . . ."

"They're starting . . ."

"Done!" Swanny exclaimed. He slumped against the pipe.

Rorq patted it. "Let's hope this baby holds," he said.

Anakin felt a drop of sweat trickle from his neck and down his back.

He heard the gush of liquid through the pipes. Swanny and Rorq kept their hands on the pipe, listening.

"That'll be the wastewater," Swanny whispered, as if Decca and her gang could hear. He patted the pipe. "The seal is holding."

"Looks like it's a go," Anakin said into his comlink. "I'm on my way."

Leaving Swanny and Rorq with the pipes, Anakin raced along the tunnels. He found Obi-Wan and Yoda hidden behind a speeder directly inside the entrance to the depot.

"They've almost finished fueling," Obi-Wan said.

Anakin saw Decca lumber into the depot and speak to her pilots. The technicians ran back and forth, replacing the heavy hoses and making last-minute checks.

The pilots left Decca and hurried to their transports.

The first pilot started up the engine. It coughed and died. The next fired his up. Another cough, a sputter, and the engine wound down. One after the other, the transport engines whined and sputtered out.

"What is happening?" Decca roared in Huttese.

"We've been sabotaged!" one of the pilots said. "Engine checklight says the fuel tanks have a foreign substance in them."

"Granta has double-crossed me!" Decca bellowed.

"Ah," Yoda murmured. "Suspicion among thieves, one can count on always."

Decca turned to the Kamarian by her side. "Send the seeker droid. We'll find that slimy monkey-lizard and take every weapon he has. We'll crush him!"

"Time I think to take the speeder," Yoda said.

Obi-Wan slipped into the pilot seat while Yoda hopped in behind and Anakin jumped in the passenger side. They kept their heads low. Obi-Wan started the engine and quietly zoomed out of the depot. He idled outside, and the seeker droid appeared a moment later. It darted down the tunnel like a fast-moving bird.

Obi-Wan gunned the motor, and they took off. It was easy to keep the seeker droid in their sights. Decca could not move very fast, but no doubt she was gathering her troops to follow the trail of the seeker wherever it ended up.

The seeker suddenly slowed, so Obi-Wan did the same. It hung in the air, which meant it was keeping its target in sight without alerting him to its presence. Obi-Wan glided to a stop, and they jumped out of the speeder.

They hurried along the few remaining meters. The tunnel curved ahead. Omega must be somewhere beyond the curve.

Walking slowly and cautiously now, they rounded the corner. They had come to a large landing area. The doors were slid back into the walls, revealing the large open space. Omega stood talking to a man dressed in heavy armor.

Anakin saw rows upon rows of bins marked with their contents. Fléchette launchers. Flamethrowers. Missile tubes. There were enough weapons here to mount an invasion.

Which, of course, was the point.

"A troop of battle droids and some guards," Obi-Wan murmured. "Nothing we can't handle."

"Prepared for this, he was not," Yoda said.

The seeker buzzed closer. Suddenly, a shadow moved, and blaster fire erupted. The seeker exploded into shards of metal.

"Got it," Feeana said. "Looks like we have company. Just as I told you."

From behind Feeana, the battle droids appeared, rolling into attack formation. First one line, then another, and another. A grenade launcher rolled into place.

Omega smiled, and Anakin realized that he had known they were coming.

Feeana had betrayed them.

CHAPTER FIFTEEN

Obi-Wan saw at once they were hopelessly outnumbered. Behind the attack droids row after row of gang soldiers appeared, all of them armed with repeating blasters. They wouldn't lack for additional weaponry. It was piled up around them.

Behind his troops, Omega stood on a gravsled with Feeana. Omega's arms were crossed, as if in expectation of a staged battle for his pleasure, and a slight smile was on his face.

"Do we have a plan?" Anakin asked hopefully.

Yoda drew his lightsaber. "Time for strategy, it is not. Time for battle, it is."

Obi-Wan felt the Force move, a giant wave that propelled him forward into the room. He caught the flow and felt it charge his first move, a devastating sweep at five attack droids at once. He cut a swath through them all and they clattered to the floor, smoking.

Omega's smile slipped, just a fraction.

Yoda had moved forward with Obi-Wan and Anakin, but his style was less dramatic than Obi-Wan's sweeps and Anakin's whirling lightsaber. His arm barely seemed to move; his attacks seemed more flicks than stabs. Yet ten attack droids were on the floor in a heap of twisted metal.

Obi-Wan saw the heavy durasteel containers suddenly move, floating up in the air, propelled by Yoda's use of the Force. As they hung above, the hinged lids opened, and flamethrowers spilled out in a fiery arc. Spewing fire, they rained down on the rest of the weapons. The blast of discharged explosives filled the air, smoke rose, and the remaining cache of weapons fused from the intense heat.

The line of gang soldiers stumbled back from the fiery spectacle, coughing from the acrid smoke. They wavered.

"Forward!" Omega screamed.

"Gladly," Obi-Wan said, and he charged forward, Anakin and Yoda at his side. Their lightsabers were hums of glowing energy. The Force moved, and droids went flying. The others were reduced to scrap. They mowed through the second line of droids, and then the next.

The soldiers stumbled backward. Some began to flee.

"Hold the line!" Omega shouted. Then he turned his back and leaped off the gravsled.

Obi-Wan saw Yoda lift his hand and send a trio of attack droids smashing against the wall. Even Anakin now was using a Force push to clear his path to attack the next line of droids. Obi-Wan had time to admire his Padawan's form, balance, and concentration. Clearly, Yoda's summoning of the Force had brought something out in Anakin. He was fighting more brilliantly than Obi-Wan had ever seen.

So Obi-Wan felt confident in leaving him with Yoda to finish off the droids. Omega was about to escape.

He gathered the Force and leaped, clearing the attack lines of droids and sailing over the retreating gang soldiers, who did not bother to try to stop him.

A hundred meters ahead, Feeana was facing what appeared to be a smooth tunnel wall made of a plastoid material. She pressed something at the side, and a recessed door slid open. Omega and Feeana disappeared inside. The door slid shut behind them.

Obi-Wan raced toward it. He did not bother to search for the release, but plunged his lightsaber into the plastoid wall. He cut a hole in seconds and pushed his way through.

He found himself in what was obviously meant one day to be a transit tunnel. It had been blasted out of rock, but the job had not been completed. Razor-sharp shards of rock jutted out from the sides of the tunnel.

A small, sleek silver cruiser was parked in a flat area ahead. Obi-Wan did not recognize the make, but it was clear to him that Omega would be able to fly above-ground and then blast out of Mawan airspace into the galaxy. He would escape again. He was seconds away from doing it. Even now, he was accessing the cockpit shell to climb in, Feeana at his heels.

Not this time.

"Always have a second exit plan," Omega said as he stood inside the craft, the cockpit dome still raised. "My father taught me that."

Something about the expression on Omega's face stopped Obi-Wan from moving forward. Omega would sacrifice Feeana in order to escape. Obi-Wan knew it, Omega knew it. The only one who didn't know it was Feeana. She was still on the hull of the ship, impatiently waiting for Omega to move so she could slide into the passenger seat.

Obi-Wan was also puzzled. In his investigation of Omega's background, he had learned that Omega never knew his father.

"Surprised?" Omega said. He was almost drawling

now, as if he had all the time in the world. "I had reasons to keep my father's identity a secret. But I think it's time I had the pleasure of telling you. I am the son of Xanatos of Telos."

Xanatos! Obi-Wan felt as though he had been struck. The former Padawan of Qui-Gon's who had turned to the dark side. Qui-Gon's greatest enemy. Obi-Wan had seen the evil that Xanatos had done. Xanatos had even invaded the Temple and tried to kill Yoda.

"You killed my father," Omega said. "He was greater than his Master, and Qui-Gon couldn't bear it, so he killed him — with your help."

"He killed himself," Obi-Wan said. "He jumped into a toxic pool on Telos rather than be captured by Qui-Gon. Qui-Gon tried to save him."

"My father would never have killed himself!" Omega shouted.

"You have spent your life constructing your own brand of truth," Obi-Wan said. "But it is not the real truth."

"Granta, let me in," Feeana said, an edge of pleading to her voice. "We have to get out of here!"

"My father protected me," Omega said. "He told me tales of the Jedi and the Temple and how they misunderstood the Force." A bitterness crept into his tone. "He had hoped that I would inherit his gift. But he knew when I was an infant that I would never be Force-sensitive."

Obi-Wan saw the opening. He saw the pain in Omega. "And he was disappointed," he said.

"He left me his company!" Omega burst out, as if he were bragging. As if his father had left him something better than love, better than approval. "He left me his fortune in Offworld."

Offworld was the corporation that Xanatos had formed, a mining operation that had used slaves and bribes and violence to build its wealth. Omega didn't create his wealth out of nothing. He had started with it.

Obi-Wan wanted to kick himself down the tunnel. He should have guessed! He should have known that beneath the jibes and insults there was something personal, something bitter, in the way Omega felt about him and the Jedi. He should have known!

He had the clues — why else would Sano Sauro pluck the promising boy away and send him to school? Sauro was hardly a benefactor to the poor. Sauro had known Xanatos well, had operated himself on Telos. And then there was the mystery of the boy's origins — why else were the mother and son on Nierport Seven, a moon that was basically a refueling stop? They were hiding, of course. Xanatos had sent them there. And after he died, they didn't have the resources to leave.

Omega blamed Obi-Wan for his father's death. He was bitter that he did not inherit his father's gift. So he would chase the Force all over the galaxy. He would grow even wealthier than his father had been. He would prove to a man no longer living that he was worthy.

Now Obi-Wan even saw Xanatos in his son. The eyes with the metallic glint of blue durasteel. The thick black hair.

He had every clue, and he had missed it.

"You are just like your Master," Omega sneered. "My father told me about Qui-Gon, how he held him back. You do the same with Anakin. Control is what you seek, and you hide it behind Jedi lessons." He spat the word "Jedi" like a curse. "Why don't you let him be himself? Why don't you show him what power he can have?"

Obi-Wan didn't have to turn. The Force hummed in the tunnel, and he knew Anakin was behind him. Anakin had heard everything.

"It ends here, Omega," Obi-Wan said.

"It will never end until you are dead," Omega said. He reached out and grabbed Feeana's ankles. With a quick, powerful thrust, he threw her off the hull of the ship. Screaming, Feeana flew in midair, straight for the jagged, knife-edged rocks.

Anakin leaped. The Force added distance and precision. He caught Feeana in his arms just millimeters from the pointed shards, twisting in midair in order to land safely.

Obi-Wan, too, had leaped, trying to land on the cruiser hull. But he had to swerve to avoid Anakin, and Omega had already gunned the engine. He took off, the cockpit dome still unengaged. Obi-Wan landed badly and fell to one knee.

The cockpit dome slid down. The cruiser gained speed.

Omega had escaped again.

CHAPTER SIXTEEN

Anakin watched as his Master rose. A heaviness seemed to lie on Obi-Wan, a weariness Anakin had never seen before.

He kept a firm grip on Feeana, who was staring down the tunnel in shock, amazed that she had been left behind.

Anakin knew that all his questions were in his eyes. He had heard of Xanatos. Every Jedi student had heard the story of the Temple invasion. Obi-Wan had told him a little of it. Now Anakin realized how much more there was to know.

"We will discuss this later, Anakin," Obi-Wan said. "We have a mission to complete."

When they emerged back into the substation, the battle was over. Decca was just arriving with her troops.

They were staring in disbelief at the litter of broken droids, fused weapons, captured forces, and only three Jedi.

Obi-Wan stepped over a pile of droids to speak to Yoda. "Omega has escaped. What should we do now with Decca?"

"A little reason now we shall use," Yoda said. "A dead end, she has come to. Listen now, she will."

He moved forward to talk to Decca.

"I thought you would lose," Feeana said numbly to Anakin. "I was afraid for my troops. I had had some dealings with Granta. He always said I could join him. He said he would protect me and my gang. I was such a fool."

There was nothing to say, Anakin saw. He led Feeana to sit with the other prisoners and then returned to Obi-Wan.

"So your vision was true," Obi-Wan said. "Yaddle met her death here. We just did not know how to interpret it."

Anakin nodded. A lump rose in his throat. Why did having the vision make him feel so responsible?

"And yet it was not true, as well," Obi-Wan said. "The vision was not about Shmi. It was about you. It was about the temptations in your life." He hesitated. "What did Omega tell you?"

Anakin hesitated and then said, "That the Jedi were holding me back. That I could free the slaves on Tatooine, free my mother. He said he would help me do it."

"That must have tempted you," Obi-Wan said.

Anakin said nothing. He could not admit it, but he could not lie.

"It is all right, Anakin. It is understandable that you would want to ease your mother's life. But being a Jedi means that your ties are to all beings. You are the only Jedi with such a strong, deep tie, and it makes it harder for you. But remember, a life of service is not only about giving up. It is about giving."

"I don't believe you're holding me back," Anakin said. "I hate him for saying it."

"Hate is not an answer," Obi-Wan said. "Understanding is." He sighed. "Xanatos could twist feelings in just that way. He was a dangerous being. Just as Omega is. We'll meet him again, I'm sure of it."

Anakin was sure of it, too.

Yoda walked slowly back to them using his walking stick, his lightsaber tucked into his utility belt, his robe swinging. It was the Yoda Anakin knew best, the wise teacher, rather than the warrior. He was glad he had seen the warrior, however. He had seen how powerful Yoda was, and yet he knew somehow that he had seen only one small corner of his power.

"Leaving the planet, Decca is," Yoda said.

"How did you manage that?" Obi-Wan asked.

"Informed her I did that the Jedi are thinking of setting up a satellite Temple on Mawan," Yoda said. "Seemed to dismay her, it did."

"We're thinking of setting up a satellite Temple?" Obi-Wan asked, surprised.

"From time to time, discuss an outpost, the Council does," Yoda said. "Merely suggesting it, I was. Enough it was to convince her that it was best to leave." He blinked at Anakin. "See you do that the right diplomacy is always better than battles, young Padawan?"

Anakin nodded obediently, but something in his face must have alerted Yoda, for suddenly his gray-blue gaze grew keen. "Know you do that Yaddle's death was not your fault," he said.

"I had the vision," Anakin burst out. "I should have known!"

"And Obi-Wan and myself?" Yoda asked sharply. "Told us of the vision you did, and yet know we did not. Blame us as well, do you?"

"Of course not," Anakin said. "But things in the vision started to come true when I was with Omega. I should never have asked Yaddle to meet with him. I should have refused. I should have tried to escape."

"When you look back, lose your place on the path,

you do." Yoda's voice gentled. "Learn you will, Anakin, that stars move and stars fall, and nothing at all do they have to do with you."

Yoda walked off with his Master. Anakin was grateful for his words.

Why hadn't his Master said them? When he'd said that Yaddle's death was his fault, Obi-Wan had remained silent.

He knew in his bones that he had caused a chain of events that led to a Jedi Master's murder. Even if that didn't make him responsible, he knew it would make it hard for him to sleep at night.

The vision hadn't been wrong. The essential truth it had left him with was part of him now. He felt it inside him like a wound. It was loss. The gulf between him and Obi-Wan was wider than ever.

BORN TO BE A BOUNTY HUNTER.

When Boba Fett's father, Jango, is killed, Boba must struggle for safety—and vengeance—using his strength, his intelligence, and his father's legacy.

Alone, young Boba Fett must go forth on his path to become a bounty hunter—but first he must escape from the evil Count Dooku.